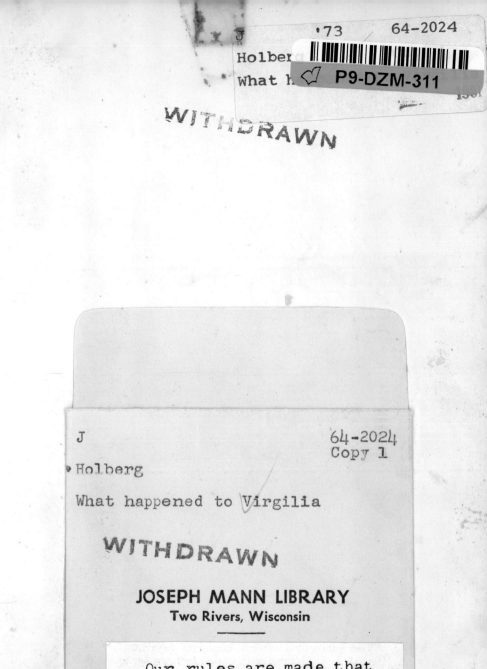

What Happened to
Virgilia

What Happened to Virgilia

By

RUTH LANGLAND HOLBERG

Illustrated by

REISIE LONETTE

Doubleday & Company, Inc.
Garden City, New York

Library of Congress Catalog Card Number 63-18232

This book is for Clare Spiewak—
Kristine, Posy, and Kathy Bruni

Chapter One

The sun in her bedroom was so bright that it forced Virgilia's eyelids open even though she wanted to keep on sleeping. She wanted to wake in her old room back in the city. It was a small, stuffy room with a narrow cot, but it was home where things didn't change, where everything was familiar.

She pushed her face into the pillow. She squeezed her eyelids tight. She tried not to smell the breeze from the open window. It was tangy with an odor of something that smelled like . . . she just had to figure out that smell. It was salty and—of course, it smelled like iodine. She lifted her head. She was awake. "No use," she mumbled to herself, and peered around the room.

Large pieces of black walnut furniture stood against the flowered wallpaper. A bureau and a table had marble tops. She looked at the rocking chair, with ruffled cushions, holding out inviting arms for a cosy retreat. There was an engraving of Lincoln on one wall. Virgilia sat up and gazed solemnly at the enormous bed with its towering headboard, marvelously carved and ornamented. She pushed down the gay patchwork quilt and stretched her feet to touch the hooked rug on the floor.

Last night when she had gone to bed in this strange room she had not seen much. The long train ride had tired her and it was very late when she had stumbled up the stairs after her aunt.

Virgilia looked at her feet resting on the pattern of a black and yellow tiger with bristling whiskers and glaring eyes.

"Not friendly, are you," she said to herself, and quoted: "Tiger! Tiger! burning bright,/In the forests of the night,/What immortal hand or eye/Could frame thy fearful symmetry?" She had loved her class in poetry—but the words seemed strange in this room.

"Virgilia?" A voice outside the door brought her to her feet. "Are you awake?"

"Yes, come in." Virgilia's mood changed and she felt shy in the presence of her father's Aunt Emma.

"Well, I declare, Virgilia, if the weather man didn't go and stop the rain. It's a fine day for you and I'm going to get the washing out on the line. Let me have your dirty clothes." Aunt Emma held out her hands.

"Oh, I'll take my things to the Laundromat, I always do," Virgilia said.

Aunt Emma snorted. "That isn't done here. We hang our things on a line to dry in the fresh air and sun. Come now, hand over your duds."

The brisk voice stirred Virgilia to sort out her clothes.

"Come down to breakfast as soon as you are washed and dressed." The lean and energetic figure bustled out of the room.

When Virgilia went down to the kitchen, the washing machine was going full tilt. "Sit down, child," Aunt Emma said. "Here's your oatmeal. I'll fry you a couple of eggs and some bacon. Or would you like pancakes with syrup right from Vermont?"

Virgilia was dumfounded. "I—I just eat dry cereal and orange juice and . . ." She didn't get a chance to say more.

"That's what's wrong with you, Virgilia. Pale as a ghost, skinny as a picked chicken, and no gumption. I'll put some meat on your bones." Aunt Emma gave her stern look.

Virgilia wasn't used to such talk. At home no one bothered about a big breakfast. Her father and mother were always in a hurry to get off to the college where they taught.

With Aunt Emma's eyes bright as a squirrel's and as watchful, Virgilia began on her oatmeal. She found that she liked its creamy texture. She liked the eggs and bacon and the muffins and steaming cup of cocoa.

"Thank you, Aunt Emma." Virgilia pushed her chair from the table and went to stand at the screen door, looking up and down the narrow, uphill street. Lately it had been named Highland Avenue after some of the newcomers had protested the old-timer's name, Dishwater Lane.

Small houses set close to the road were spanking white in the early sun. Dogs out on their daily walks, cats scrubbing themselves on doorsteps, caught her attention. She wanted to see more of the neighborhood.

"Could I go for a walk?" Virgilia's timid question brought a flash of surprise from Aunt Emma. "Goodness, child, go as far as you like. You can't get lost here in Rockport, if that worries you. Everybody knows everybody else, if you need to ask directions."

Virgilia heard the town clock strike six times. She had never been up so early in the city. "Do you always get up so early?" she ventured.

"Early? My lands!" Aunt Emma sputtered. "When

11

Jake was alive we got up at the crack of dawn. He went lobstering and brought his traps back before anyone else, and he got to the market before the other men. I'm in the habit of getting up early. Go along now."

Virgilia walked down the hill. She crossed a street and turned left on Jewett Street. It was very quiet except for the twittering of birds in the elms and a few sea gulls squawking overhead.

"How quiet it is," she thought, "and lonesome." A quick catch in her throat brought stinging tears to her eyes. "What will I do—without mother and father, with no one to tell me what I should do."

She brushed the tears away with the back of her hand and started to walk toward a glimpse of blue water far down the street.

"Oh, say, can you see, by the dawn's early light,/ What so proudly we hailed at the twilight's last gleaming?"

Virgilia stopped and listened.

"Whose broad stripes and bright stars thro' the perilous fight,/O'er the ramparts we watched were so gallantly streaming":

Virgilia came close to a tall hedge and looked between the branches. She saw a small dumpling of a woman raising the American flag on a weather-

beaten old pole. She was singing "The Star-Spangled Banner," and she was completely alone in her yard.

All the stanzas were sung. The flag rippled its red and white stripes against the clear blue sky. The singer gave it a broad smile and turned to trot into the house.

Virgilia walked to the opening of the hedge and peered at a grass-trodden path leading to the oddest house she had ever seen. It was three stories high and two of the stories backed right up against a high stone wall, while the third story was above the street which went along the top of the wall.

She stared at the porch outside the second floor. "It looks shabby," she said to herself, "and spooky, too. It looks as if it just grew. I wish I could go in and maybe find a secret room or a mystery."

Her eyes took in the neglected gardens overgrown with tall weeds and scraggy bushes. There was a tottering old woodshed just inside the hedge. Still curious, she walked along and looking back at the same time at the faded yellow house with its odd ells and dormers, she stumbled and fell hard on the pebbly street.

"My knees," she moaned, "they are skinned and bleeding." But she limped to the end of the street and made a left turn at the corner of a small public library. "Cleaves Street," she read. It was puzzling to find short streets leading into each other at unexpected turns.

"Ouch," she muttered. It hurt to bend her knees, but she walked stiffly along eager to see the back of the old yellow house ahead of her on Cleaves Street. It had a store in a one-story-appearing house. It had two fat chimneys, each with a slight bend in it as if it were tired of being battered by the stormy gales from the ocean just a short distance down the street.

Virgilia forgot her skinned knees. Here was another mystery. What kind of store would have its little windows crowded with faded old birthday cards, rubber balls, boxes of rusty jacks, a stuffed, gaily feathered bird, plants, and funny-looking dolls? She pressed close to the tiny panes. "I can't see what there is to sell in there," she said to herself.

The key turned in the door lock. It opened. "My, you are an early customer. Come in, come in. Don't stand there gawking."

It was the singer who had sung while she raised her flag. Virgilia gulped. She was embarrassed. "I—I wasn't planning to buy anything," she explained in a meek voice.

"Huh, stranger in these parts. Where d'you come from?" the voice asked.

"I come from New York State, Glenville." Seeing the look of curiosity and interest, Virgilia went on.

"I'm staying with my father's Aunt Emma on Highland Avenue."

There was a snort of laughter from the singer. "You mean Dishwater Lane. Well, go on. Where are your parents?"

Virgilia explained. Each statement brought many changes in the expression of her listener's face, and as Virgilia went on, they were mostly disapproving.

"My father teaches Latin in the college and my mother teaches art. Both have been given Fulbright Grants for a year's study in Europe," Virgilia said.

"And they left you behind?" The words were spoken with indignation.

Virgilia tried to explain. "Oh, I wouldn't fit in with their plans and it would be much too expensive to take me along. And I'd miss school so I'm to stay in Rockport for a year and go to school here." But when she spoke the word 'year,' Virgilia's face was sad.

"You poor girl. And I bet that Emma Harris isn't going to spoil you or coddle you. She's cold as a haddock, I always claimed. Being a good cook and housekeeper is all she thinks about."

The speaker shook her head from side to side. "What's your name?" she asked.

"Virgilia Stewart. My father named me for Virgil who wrote the poetry he teaches in college. My father is going to Italy where Virgil was born, a long time before Christ."

Virgilia saw the look of amazement following her information, not much of it appeared to make sense to the listener.

"Now, look here, girl. Nobody's going to call you that outlandish name made up from some ancient Italian. No, sir. From now on you are Jill."

Virgilia, newly named Jill, smiled and then she giggled. "I like that name. Thank you for naming me Jill, Mrs.—" she hesitated.

"Miss. Miss Lucy Applebird. Call me Lucy. All the folks do. Big and little, rich or poor, so you call me Lucy, too." Jill met a wide smile on the chubby, wrinkled face that somehow resembled a rosy apple. She felt a new kind of easy warmness around her heart. She was enchanted with her first friend. She didn't even feel stiff and painfully shy as she usually did with older people and even with children her own age.

Jill's brown eyes sparkled. Impulsively she burst out, "I'd love to see your store . . . Lucy."

"No sooner said than done," Lucy Applebird chuckled.

Jill crossed the worn threshold. "How tiny!" she cried. "I've never seen such a tiny store. The stores at home are all big, with parking spaces."

17

Lucy Applebird laughed. "No need for parking spaces here. My customers come on foot. They are mostly too young to drive cars."

Jill saw the battered wooden counter and on it the trays and shallow boxes of candy all protected from eager fingers by a curved glass top.

Lucy explained. "I sell penny candy and the neighbor's children learn to count from me. I help them to learn arithmetic."

Jill was fascinated. The three shelves back of the counter held packages of various kinds of cookies and crackers, but there was nothing else to sell. The store had an air of great age. It smelled dry and dusty. The woodwork was dark and worn with long service.

Jill turned to Lucy Applebird. "Is this all you sell in the store?" she asked.

"Yup," was the indignant answer. "I used to sell bread and stuff, but the firms refused to sell me small amounts a few years ago. They want big orders and I can't sell as much as the stores on Main Street."

"I'm sorry," Jill ventured.

Lucy Applebird laughed. "Oh, well, I like to take life easy. I like to play. Come along into the rough room. I'm going to clean the canary's cage."

Jill had no idea what a rough room might be. It opened off the back of the store and it was indeed a rough room. The wood had never been painted, in fact it looked like the inside of a barn.

"I like this room," Lucy said. She busied herself cleaning the canary cage. "I eat here, out of cans. Then I throw them away in the shed down on Jewett Street. I only have to wash a cup for my tea. Then, when the town collects rubbish each spring, they take the cans to the dump. Now Mrs. Allen next door has to pay the regular rubbish collector fifty cents a week. I hire no men or women. I let things go—no grass is cut and no weeds are pulled."

The canary was in his clean cage. "Come in and visit."

Lucy led the way into her living room just off the side of the store. When she moved the cage near a sunny window with plants on the sill, the canary hopped about making a cheerful noise. The faded papered wall had many old-fashioned calendars of bygone years tacked on them. They were bright scenes and some were of large-eyed angelic children with fluffy cats in their arms. Old greeting cards were pinned helter-skelter on the walls.

Lucy Applebird tucked herself into a rocking chair and beamed at Jill who took another rocking chair, seating herself gingerly. "I never sat in a rocking chair," she said. "It's nice." She gave herself a push and rocked back and forth. The visit began.

"My father declared his life was one long honeymoon. He kept the store and sold all sorts of goods. We three children were brought up in this house and do you know, Jill, it was once a dance hall near Front Beach. Papa bought it and had it moved up here and he built on to it time and again. We had such fun."

"Fun?" Jill spoke wistfully. She wondered about herself. She didn't remember having fun with her parents. They were always too busy, but she loved them dearly and now they were far away for a whole year. And she was all alone in a strange place.

Jill jumped up from the rocking chair. "I must go. Aunt Emma will think I'm lost or—or something."

"Come again, Jill." Lucy spoke with warmth. "I like company."

Lucy Applebird's voice followed Jill to the store door where a bell jingled in a shrill protest when she shut the door with a swift bang. Up the street she ran, her knees were sore but she ran right up Dishwater Lane. Aunt Emma was hanging wet clothes on the line in the back yard and she didn't see her. Jill flew up to her room and her plain little face crumpled up as she fell across the broad bed in a storm of tears. She didn't know what was the matter. She just felt awful.

Chapter Two

Two hoarse, penetrating blasts of the fire alarm brought Jill from a deep sleep. She rolled over, sat up, and then leaped from the huge bed.

It was a horrible noise. She stood, trembling and afraid. The appearance of Aunt Emma, fresh and calm-looking, with an armful of Jill's clean clothes, startled her more.

"What was that awful noise?" Jill's shaky voice made Aunt Emma look at her with surprise and she laughed. "Why, those two blows come every day at twelve o'clock noon. Now, if you want to know where a fire is when it keeps on blowing, you count the blows and look at the card on the kitchen wall. The number tells you where the fire is." Aunt Emma put Jill's clothes away in the big bureau. "We have a a volunteer fire department, they give us the best service you ever saw."

Aunt Emma stopped chatting and gave Jill a sharp look.

"You have been crying, Virgilia." Her voice was accusing. "And look at your knees. Do you hurt some place else?"

Jill said, "I fell down. It's nothing."

"Well, did you have a nice walk?" Aunt Emma was curious.

"Yes," Jill said.

"Go on, tell me all about it," Aunt Emma prodded her.

Jill saw that Aunt Emma intended to keep a close watch on her doings and she decided she might as well get used to reporting each detail. She had never had to at home because her parents were too busy to ask questions.

"I heard Lucy Applebird singing 'The Star-Spangled Banner' as she raised the flag. I was going down the street and stumbled and skinned my knees. I turned up another street and I saw the other side of her house with a tiny store at one end."

"Um hum," Aunt Emma muttered. "And she asked you to come in for a visit. Oh, she's a great talker and she'll talk the arm off you, if you let her. She told you all about her folks and how her grandfather was a Baptist minister. She thinks she knows more about the Bible than our own minister. I bet some day she is going to rise up in her pew and tell him he is wrong about some point or other."

Jill was beginning to think that Aunt Emma and Lucy Applebird were not the best of friends. "Yes, I went in the store and the rough room too," Jill admitted. "She has a canary."

Aunt Emma sniffed and curled up her lip in distaste.

"She thinks it is smart. A smart bird! My lands! She had a cat named Christopher and she had birthday parties for him, just a dratted old tomcat."

Jill thought it was time she defended Lucy. "I like her. She is going to call me Jill and not that long, serious-sounding Virgilia. She is my friend."

Aunt Emma's bright squirrel eyes snapped. "Why didn't she fix your knees if she's such a good friend? I guess she never noticed them, she is so busy talking about herself and her folks. You come along to the bathroom and I'll show you where the antiseptic is and the Band-Aids. Then you come down to dinner."

Jill sighed. She wasn't used to such excitement.

The afternoon passed with a marketing errand on Main Street. Aunt Emma showed her off to her acquaintances. A girl from a big city, she bragged, until Jill began to wonder if there were any girls of her own age that Aunt Emma knew.

Back in Dishwater Lane (Jill called it that to herself) she sat on the front steps with a book she had brought from home.

"Hi!" someone called.

Jill looked up. There was a chubby girl pushing a doll buggy up the lane. There wasn't a doll in it. It was filled with a neat pile of newspapers.

"Here's your paper."

The girl handed Jill a copy of the Gloucester *Daily Times.*

"Thank you," Jill murmured. She felt shy. The girl regarded Jill solemnly for a moment. "Are you here for the summer?"

Jill made an effort to be polite. She didn't respond to the other's evident desire to get acquainted.

"No," Jill answered. Then seeing the girl waiting for her to go on, she said, "I am staying here for a year."

"A year? A whole year? Then you aren't summer folks. Why are you here?" The questioner persisted until Jill was forced to give her an explanation.

"My parents are in Europe for a year, and they are doing research. I wouldn't fit in with their plans."

The girl came to sit beside Jill on the step. Her interest was intense, her bright blue eyes stared at Jill as if she were a fascinating and most unusual person of great importance.

Jill went on, "My father teaches Latin in a college

25

and my mother teaches art. Both have Fulbright Grants and that means they are very high up in their work and they are given money to study further in their chosen fields."

The other girl blinked. This was something she had never heard of. She leaned closer. "What's your name? How old are you? Will you go to school and live with Mrs. Harris? Is she related to you?" The rapid fire of questions made Jill giggle. Suddenly both girls were laughing together. Jill found herself answering all of the questions.

"It's my turn now. You tell me about yourself." She smiled at the chubby, blue-eyed paper girl.

"Well, my name is Patricia Wentworth and I'm called Pat. I am going on eleven years, just like you. I have this paper route so I can earn money. I'm saving it."

"What for?" Jill was interested.

"Oh, that's a secret," Pat muttered. "Something I'm wishing and wishing for."

Pat looked at Jill. "Have you a secret? Something special you are wishing for?"

Jill was thoughtful, wondering what she would like more than anything else in the world. A thought popped into her mind. She would like a best friend. A wonderful friend who would be fun, and. . . . Jill thrust the thought out of her mind. It would never come true. Girls didn't like her very much. She would not think about it.

"I don't have a secret," she told Pat, regretfully.

Aunt Emma came to the door. "Hand me the paper, Virgilia. It is late. No wonder with the paper girl dawdling on her route."

Pat rose quickly. She trundled the heavy doll buggy up the lane. "Good-by Jill, be seeing you!" she yelled back.

"Now you come in to supper, Virgilia. After supper you can wipe dishes. Your pa said for you to be useful and to help around the house." Aunt Emma held the door open. Jill went into the front hall.

"Look here." Aunt Emma bent over the seat of the hall tree. She lifted the top. "I put your overshoes in here."

Jill peered in at the collection of old-fashioned black rubbers and huge galoshes. "Oh, I see my rain boots. I'll remember where they are, thank you." Jill watched the lid fall with a slam.

"Rain boots. A fancy new name for overshoes," Aunt Emma said. "Now here are the umbrellas at this side with a basin to catch drips from the rain." Aunt Emma put her hand on one with a reddish curved handle. "This one is cherry wood and it smells sweet in rainy weather. It was Jake's. He didn't mind rain, being a lobster man, except on Sundays—he was funny that way." Aunt Emma smiled tenderly.

Jill drew a deep breath. She felt stretched inside. So many new experiences had happened to her that she seemed too small to take them all in. She needed time to get used to her new life in Rockport.

The next morning Jill wiped dishes for Aunt Emma and put them away in the long, narrow, cool pantry. It had a small window at the end and it smelled spicy, like ginger cookies. When she returned to the kitchen she saw a man standing at the screen door. "Fish today, Mrs. Harris?" he called, and peered through the screen.

"Oh," he said. "Who are you?"

Jill told him that she was staying with Mrs. Harris, who was her father's aunt. She realized again that the people in Rockport were inquisitive and wanted to know all about strangers.

Aunt Emma came into the kitchen with a dust cloth in her hand. "I thought I heard voices. Oh, it's you, Charlie Nelson. I'll have a medium-sized haddock. This is chowder day." She turned to Jill. "Take a big plain plate from the pantry and get the haddock."

Jill went to the pantry and found a large plate. She took it out to the road where a small truck was parked. It had a homemade compartment in the body of the truck, and the fish man had its lid raised and was weighing a fish on a scale. Jill held out the plate and the fish was laid on it, the tail and head hung over the edges.

"How much is it?" Aunt Emma called from the door.

"Sixty cents," the fish man yelled back. Jill took the plate to the door and Aunt Emma gave her the money for the fish. Going down to the truck Jill noticed a very large, smooth-haired white dog sitting on the seat. She reached up to pat him.

"What's your dog's name?" she asked, when the fish man climbed up to push the dog aside to make room for himself.

"His name is Babo and he isn't my dog. He waits for me on High Street and comes along just for the ride. A man on Hale Street named him Babo because he looks so clean. I don't know his real name."

The dog barked. The fish man chuckled. "There is a cat who always waits for me in the red house up the hill. Babo sees her coming to get fish scraps." The truck started and he called back, "Be seeing you." He grinned at Jill and she smiled a small smile. She had to smile too, because shopping was so different from city shopping. She wasn't used to smiling at people she didn't know, but the fish man took it for granted that she was friendly.

Aunt Emma had a fish chowder for noon dinner. Jill tasted it suspiciously, sure that she would not like it. But soon she was spooning up cubes of potatoes and chunks of fish from the creamy depths of her bowl. Crisp, thick chowder crackers and sour pickles accompanied the chowder.

"Virgilia," Aunt Emma began. "I made your bed today. Tomorrow you can make it yourself. Keep your room neat and your clothes picked up."

"I will try to be neat, Aunt Emma. It is such a large room, I never had enough places for my books and stuff at home, my room was so small. I like having lots of room," Jill said.

"What are you going to do this afternoon?" Aunt Emma asked.

"I don't know," Jill said. "Could I go to the public library and take out some books?"

"Didn't you bring enough books with you? You've got a box full of them." Aunt Emma said.

"Yes, but I read fast and I like to go to libraries and see what they have on the shelves," Jill told her.

"Well, go along. The library is just down where Cleaves Street and Jewett Street meet." Aunt Emma bustled around the kitchen. The dishes were washed and wiped and put away. Jill went down the hill and when she came to Lucy Applebird's store, she stopped to read a note pinned on the door. GONE SWIMMING, it said.

She lingered at the windows looking at the many articles displayed inside. Someone else stopped beside her, and a boy's snicker brought her to turn and stare at him. They eyed each other with interest. "You're new here," he finally offered.

Jill nodded and said nothing, too shy to talk.

"Well—" he began slowly. "What are you hanging around here for, can't you read that sign? Lucy's gone swimming."

Jill spoke up. "I can read. I'm simply looking at the queer doll standing there." She pointed. The boy gave it a glance. "That is a Kewpie doll, kids had them years ago."

"Oh," Jill murmured. The silence between them grew embarrassing. The boy continued to stare at her. "Where are you going?" he began again. Jill realized that he was like all the other Rockporters she had met. He wanted to know all about her. She tried to overcome her reluctance to talk to a stranger.

"I'm going to the library," she said.

"It isn't open today," the boy told her.

There was a heavy silence.

"When is it open?" Jill asked.

"Tuesdays, Thursdays, and Saturdays till five

o'clock, except on Saturdays when it stays open until nine," he said.

They continued their awkward conversation for a few minutes, when Lucy Applebird broke in on them.

"The water is cold today." She shivered.

Jill eyed her in amazement. The small, round figure wore a bathing suit with a deep ruffle sewed around the bottom edge. It covered her knees. She had a frayed terry-cloth robe hanging over her shoulders and a rubber cap came down low, hiding all her hair.

"You want anything in the store, Tommy?" she asked the boy. He said no, he had just been going by. Lucy nodded. "And you saw Jill here and wanted to know her."

Tommy got red in the face and the redness showed through his large crop of freckles.

"Let me make you two properly acquainted. Jill Stewart from New York, Tommy Andrews. His father is town treasurer." Lucy beamed on them.

Jill managed a smile and a nod. Tommy scratched his stubby crew cut and shuffled his feet and grinned at Jill. He gulped, and finally stuttered, "Say, do you—a—want to go swimming—this afternoon?"

Jill's brown eyes flew wide open with surprise. No

boy had ever asked her to go to a movie or skating or to a game or anything.

"I'll have to ask Aunt Emma," she faltered.

"Oh, shucks," Lucy Applebird broke in. "You go ahead and get into your bathing suit and meet here. Emma Harris won't mind. You tell her, if she says anything, that I say you are to go to the beach with Tommy Andrews."

Jill was excited and eager to get into her swim suit. Aunt Emma wasn't around the house, and in a jiffy Jill was back at the store waiting for Tommy who came in a few minutes. The beach was in the center of town right down in back of the Main Street stores.

"Can you swim?" Tommy asked her. They stood on a broad, sandy beach.

"I learned swimming in the gym pool but I have never been in salt water." She shivered and hugged herself. The waves lapped at her feet.

Tommy plunged into the water and yelled back, "The water's fine, come on in."

There were many swimmers, young and old, splashing and swimming and wading in the water. Their joyful cries exhilarated Jill; she took a deep breath and ran into the water and swam with so little effort that she was surprised. She kept on swimming until Tommy said she ought not to stay in too long.

33

They came out and lay on the warm sand. Other
girls and boys joined them, each curious about Jill.
Their interest and friendliness soon overcame Jill's
shyness and she was happy to have Tommy tell them
that she was a fine swimmer. Jill added, "This is the
first time I have been in salt water. I like it better
than fresh water, it seems to hold you up."

One of the girls told her that the old stone quarries
were filled with water for those who liked fresh,
warmer water. Soon the group broke up and Jill and

Tommy left the beach together. Walking up Cleaves
Street, Lucy Applebird's fantastic house, with its fat,
crooked chimney, stood out from its sober, everyday
neighboring houses.

Jill pointed to a sort of tower on top of the roof.
"I wonder what is in that attic?" She turned to
Tommy. "Maybe there is a secret, hidden room, with
a mystery in it."

Tommy hooted. "It is just a crazy old house. Artists
paint it every summer. Classes sit along Cleaves

35

Street and by the middle of summer you can hardly drive a car through. I don't see why they paint such a hideous old house."

Jill spoke up. "I'd paint it if I knew how to paint. It is like something out of Grimms' fairy tales."

"Pooh," Tommy snorted. "Do you read such junk?"

Jill flashed back. "Fairy tales are not junk. They are ancient folk tales handed down from generation to generation."

"Hey!" Tommy stood still. "You look sort of cute when you get mad, your eyes get so bright."

Jill shrugged her shoulders and made a face. Tommy teased her. "I didn't know you had such spunk. Keep it up."

They had reached the beginning of Highland Avenue, where Jill turned off.

"Be seeing you," Tommy called, and ran into Broadway.

Jill hurried up the street. She was chilly and her suit was damp. Her hair dripped down her back in a lank pony tail. No one was home. After dressing, Jill sat on the front steps to wait for Pat, the paper girl, to push her doll buggy full of the Gloucester *Daily Times*, up Dishwater Lane. Jill smiled dreamily. She wanted to tell Pat about Tommy Andrews.

Chapter Three

Pat was late. When she finally came puffing up to the Harris house, Jill said, "Hello Pat, come and sit down awhile."

Pat said, "I can't. I have to collect for this week." She opened the Harris mailbox and fumbled around until she brought out forty-two cents in change. She put it in a small, stout bag and stuffed it in the doll buggy. The Gloucester *Daily Times* was handed to Jill.

Jill looked disappointed. Pat eyed her with interest. "What did you do today?"

"That is what I wanted to tell you about," Jill mumbled. She was shy, suddenly. She thought perhaps Pat wasn't feeling as friendly as she was yesterday. She brightened when Pat said, "I deliver the Saturday papers in the early morning. It is a new ar-

38

rangement so the people who write and print the paper can have a week end for doing other things."

Pat started to push the doll buggy up the hill. "I'll come to see you after dinner and let's do something together. Be seeing you." Her cheerful voice drifted back.

Jill sat in the late sun drying her damp hair. When Aunt Emma came home from a meeting of the Rug and Quilt Club, she said, "Well, I see you've been swimming. Did you go alone?"

"I went with Tommy Andrews. Lucy Applebird introduced us," Jill said. "It is the first time I ever swam in salt water and I liked it. I'm going to swim out to the raft and dive the next time."

"That's good. Better for you than hunching over a book." Aunt Emma heaved a heavy work bag into the house and dumped it on the hall-tree seat. "I don't know as I have much appetite for supper. We had tea and sandwiches and some of Mrs. Andrews' fine applesauce cake. She is a good cook."

"Is she Tommy's mother?" Jill asked, and Aunt Emma nodded. Jill hoped Aunt Emma would have a good supper. She felt hungry after swimming.

The supper was bountiful and Jill noticed Aunt Emma ate cold ham and potato salad as if she had a sharp appetite after all.

"Virgilia," Aunt Emma said. "Bring that box of dry

beans from the pantry. I'll put them to soak over-
night. I hope you like baked beans. I always bake my
own for Saturday night. We have left-over beans and
codfish cakes for breakfast on Sunday with blueberry
muffins if the berries are in season."

Jill hated beans. Her mother opened cans of beans
and heated them in a pan. Frankfurters sometimes
were served with the beans. Jill wasn't fond of them
either.

Dishes were washed, the television set was turned
on, and Aunt Emma settled down for an evening's
entertainment. She could knit and watch the pictures
almost at the same time, Jill noticed. Jill listened and
looked and dozed in her chair until bedtime.

On Saturday Jill waited for Pat to arrive. It was
midafternoon before she appeared and Jill had decided sadly that Pat really had not meant to come at
all.

"Hi!" Pat chirped in her jolly voice. "I had so much
to do at home and my mother needs me to stay with
the kids while she goes to Gloucester to shop. So
you come home with me."

Jill hesitated. She wasn't used to making up her
mind quickly. She felt bashful about meeting Pat's
family. "I'll ask Aunt Emma. I'm not sure what she
will say." Jill almost hoped she would say no.

"Go and ask her quick," Pat urged.

Jill went into the house slowly. She was disappointed because she had wanted Pat to stay. However, Aunt Emma was pleased with Pat's invitation. "You go right along, Virgilia. The Wentworths are nice people. Come home for supper."

Pat and Jill started out for Summer Street, where Pat lived in a snug little house with a large, old, weather-beaten barn in back. The house was bursting with children, younger than Pat. She pointed them out. "Joey, Elizabeth, and Paul are there. The twins are Mavis and Maude."

Jill was amazed. The children were friendly and rushed to show Jill their treasures. The twins smiled and drooled and waved hands and feet, and there was such an air of contentment in the house that Jill soon felt at ease. Pat drew her into a small bedroom she shared with Elizabeth. "Look at my collection, Jill." She pointed to the pictures of horses pinned on the wall. "I've got a big box full of horse pictures. I keep it under the bed. I'll show them to you."

The girls sat on the floor while Pat drew out newspaper clippings about horses and colored magazine pictures of horses. Jill was speechless. It began to dawn on her that Pat was mad about horses. Jill had taken a few riding lessons at home, but she was afraid of horses and did not enjoy her lessons and, since her parents didn't care, she had stopped the lessons.

41

Now she wished she knew more about horses because Pat liked them so much.

Pat whispered, "Shall I tell you my secret wish? Will you promise not to tell a soul?"

Jill's brown eyes were wide with speculation. "I promise not to tell," she whispered back. Pat drew out a page of ads from the Gloucester *Daily Times*.

"Read this." She pointed to a column. Jill read aloud, "Hot-water heater, like new . . ."

"Oh, no," Pat cried. "This one."

Jill read: "Horse, handsome, iron-gray, middle-aged horse, excellent disposition, a pet. Good wind and work, excellent riding horse. Must have a good home. Price $150. Charles A. Putnam, 398 Maple St., Danvers."

Jill turned to Pat whose face was bright with delight. "Oh, I'd love to own that horse, I'd give him a good home. I wish for a horse more than anything in the whole wide world."

Jill said, "A hundred and fifty dollars is a lot of money."

Pat groaned, "I know, that is the trouble. I don't have that much money and my dad has nothing to spare."

Jill looked at the top of the paper. "But Pat, this ad came out in April, more than a month ago. The horse is probably sold by now."

Pat looked sorrowful. "Maybe not," she murmured. "Oh, I wish I had a horse, I wish it so much that it hurts. I keep thinking I'll write to that man and ask if he still has the horse."

She put her pictures back in the box. "Jill, will you help me to write the letter?"

"Of course," Jill said.

Pat ran out of the room and came back with a box of stationery and a pencil. Jill helped her to compose the letter.

Dear Mr. Putnam;

I wish to know if you still have that iron-gray horse for sale. I would like to buy it but I do not have enough money. I could pay down $19.75 and I would pay the rest each week. I earn $12 a week for delivering papers. I would be kind and I would love the horse very much.

Your friend,
Patricia Wentworth.

P.S. We have a barn and a stall for a horse.

Your friend,
Patricia Wentworth.
33 Summer Street, Rockport, Mass.

"There," Pat said, and sealed the letter and stamped it. "You drop it in the mailbox when you go home, Jill."

It was soon time to go home. Pat's mother was back, and she was just like Pat, cheerful and energetic. Then Mr. Wentworth came home from the Finnish baths, and the children clustered around him until each was hugged and kissed in turn. He even kissed Jill who was flustered with surprise. Her parents never made such a loving fuss about her.

Pat waved good-by, and Jill walked down Summer Street. She dropped Pat's letter in a corner mailbox. "I hope Mr. Putnam answers the letter," she said to herself. She wanted so much for Pat to get her secret wish.

Aunt Emma had supper ready. The chubby brown bean pot steamed and sent out a hearty aroma that Jill sniffed. "Smells good," she said to herself. "But I don't like beans."

Aunt Emma ladled out a mound of beans onto her plate. There was warm brown bread, sticky with plump raisins, and there was piccalilli and there were thin slices of pale pink ham left from lunch.

Gingerly, Jill tasted the beans. She took a second forkful and then another. "I like your baked beans," she admitted to Aunt Emma.

"I suppose you have been brought up on canned beans," Aunt Emma said. "Some canned foods are all right, but give me beans baked for hours in a slow oven with a dollop of molasses and an onion buried in the bottom of the pot and slices of salt pork on top."

Jill said, "When you talk about cooking, I get hungry. You make food sound so good."

"We'll wash your hair tonight, Virgilia, and I will rub it dry for you." Aunt Emma started to clear the table and Jill helped her. They went up to the bathroom and Aunt Emma scrubbed and soaped Jill's hair and rinsed it again and again. Jill liked the feeling of the strong fingers rubbing her hair dry with a towel. She brushed it until it began to shine.

With her soft hair spread over her pillow, Jill sank into the wide bed and fell asleep at once.

Jill's first Sunday in Rockport commenced with the ringing of church bells. Three churches near by had bells that rang with vigorous pullings on the ropes by three sextons. The other churches did not have bell towers. Aunt Emma's hearty breakfast over, Jill was given orders to put on a nice dress and hat for church. "No slacks or shorts on Sundays," she told Jill.

The walk to Aunt Emma's church was through the old part of the town. Jill thought the lofty green elms and the clipped lawns were lovely. The white churches had flickering shadows playing over them. It made her feel quiet and pensive.

The first person to greet Jill was Lucy Applebird,

who bounced ahead of them with determination to get into her usual pew. Jill wondered if this might be the morning she would rise up and declare that her interpretation of the Scriptures was not in accordance with the preacher's. This was something Aunt Emma feared.

Jill shared Aunt Emma's hymnbook and she sang with such a clear, sweet voice that Aunt Emma gave her a warm smile. After church she said, "Virgilia, you ought to be in the choir. You saw that the choir had mixed ages."

Jill shrank into herself. "Oh, I couldn't. I wouldn't like to sit up in front of all the people and sing."

"Nonsense," declared Aunt Emma. "I'm going to speak to the choirmaster about you."

Jill felt miserable. She simply would not sing in the choir with people looking at her.

After dinner Jill said she was going to change into her shorts. "It is so warm today," she explained.

"Virgilia, I said no shorts or slacks on Sundays. Besides, we are going to call on my cousin, Mary Littlefield."

Jill did not feel like visiting strangers. She wanted to read. She had planned to write a letter to her parents, instead of making a call. But she found the walk through short, twisting streets to Cousin Mary's

47

on Hale Street, picturesque and quiet. Jill remarked on the quietness of town.

"Wait till next month, the cars in this town! Where they come from and where they go, beats me," Aunt Emma complained.

They came to a corner house and Aunt Emma raised the knocker on the wide door.

"Come in!" a friendly voice called. They entered, and were greeted by a young black cocker spaniel, who pawed them joyfully.

"Down, Opie!" a man's voice called.

Jill loved the dog's affectionate leaping. While the older people visited, Jill was sent to the back yard with Opie and Polly, the cat. "Oh, your cat lost her tail!" she cried out.

Cousin Mary explained, "No, she was born that way. All her family were born without tails; see, she has just a little nubbin instead of a tail."

"My," Jill said to herself. "Rockport is certainly different from home in every way. Even cats without tails."

The afternoon passed with chatting about relatives and friends, and Jill had to tell all over again about her parents and their Fulbright Grants. Glasses of lemonade and cookies were brought out to the terrace. Opie was spanked after he snatched a cooky from Jill's hand. "He is a young dog and doesn't know any better," Cousin Mary apologized for Opie.

Jill was beginning to enjoy herself. Cousin Mary and her husband promised to take her swimming to Good Harbor Beach in Gloucester. They told her it was a long, smooth stretch of silvery sand with no stones, even when the tide was out.

On the way home Jill decided that the older people were friendly and nice, but she wanted friends of her own age. Now that she knew Pat and Tommy, it seemed more exciting and interesting to have friends of her own age. "I hope they like me," she said to herself.

After supper she wrote a letter to her parents. She told them about Aunt Emma and about swimming in salt water. She was going to tell them about Pat, the paper girl, and her doll buggy that she used to haul papers in, but that might sound silly to them. She ended up saying she liked Aunt Emma's cooking and she was helping her with the dishes and taking care of her own room. "Write soon, your daughter, Virgilia Stewart."

She sealed it and stuck a stamp on it. She went downstairs and asked, "Where shall I mail my letter?"

"Leave it in the hall. In the morning you can take it to the post office and at the same time you can buy a box of Fig Newtons in Lucy Applebird's store. Don't you want to look at television?" she added.

Jill sat down and tried to interest herself in a drama that kept Aunt Emma's eyes glued to the screen. But the picture faded away and, the next thing she knew, Aunt Emma was shaking her. "Wake up, Virgilia."

"I fell asleep." Jill rubbed her eyes.

"It happens to everybody who stays in Rockport a few days. The sea air lets them down and they sleep like babies any hour of the day or night," Aunt Emma said.

Jill yawned. She could hardly get up the stairs and to bed. She shut her eyes. Her last thought was, "I'm going to ask Lucy Applebird about that room at the top of her house. It doesn't have a window and it sticks up by itself from the roof . . ." Then she was sound asleep.

Chapter Four

Jill had a dream in the night and she tried to remember it while she was walking along to Lucy Applebird's store.

"I remember being in her house and I was trying to scream because I was frightened. I woke up because I was thrashing around in my bed and I couldn't get to sleep for a long time," Jill said to herself. She looked at Lucy's house with its odd tower. "It was something about that room up there." She remembered that, but nothing more came to her mind. The place looked as usual. She opened the door, the bell tinkled, and Lucy Applebird came into the store, and got her a box of Fig Newtons. A small boy came in with a fistful of pennies and Lucy helped him count out five pennies. He went off with a bag of candy.

"I teach them to count, you see." Lucy Applebird stood behind the counter. "What are you up today, Jill?" she asked.

"Oh, nothing," Jill said.

"Come in and visit." Lucy invited her into a little hall. A door in it led to Cleaves Street. "I never use this door. I have enough doors in this house."

Jill saw another door. "Does this go upstairs?" she asked.

Lucy nodded. "I don't use the upstairs rooms. I never go up there except to close the scuttle if it rains, or to open it when the weather is fair."

"What sort of tower is on top of the house?" Jill asked.

"That isn't a tower, it's just a bump or swelling on the house. Papa never got around to finishing another story on the house. Now don't you get romantic and think it is a tower."

"But," Jill began. She wanted to find out more about it. Lucy acted strangely. She pushed Jill back into the store. "I remember I have something to do down the street. I can't visit today."

Jill was almost forced out of the store and she heard the key turn in the lock. She thought Lucy Applebird's face had a troubled and sad expression.

"She acted as if she had seen a ghost." Jill pondered. "She changed and she wanted me to leave."

Jill was puzzled and dismayed. "I should not have been curious and asked questions."

Jill felt more strongly than ever that there was a mystery and secret in that house. She looked back and saw Lucy Applebird wearing a hat and coat, waiting on Broadway for the Gloucester bus. She had not gone down to Main Street at all.

Jill crossed to the post office on Broadway to mail her letter. The police station and the fire station were next to it. Coming down the post office steps, she realized how near Lucy's house was, on the Jewett Street side. She crossed the street and went on a footpath between the Methodist church and the town hall. The American flag was streaming from the top of its flagpole as it did every day in Lucy Applebird's yard.

Jill went along home. "Aunt Emma," she asked later, "does Lucy Applebird have friends in Gloucester? She just got on the Gloucester bus."

"No, I never heard of anybody in particular, but Lucy is odd. Every now and then she locks the store and nobody knows what she does in Gloucester. She doesn't go to her cousin's house. They all fight with each other except when there is a funeral.

"Then they get together and have a great time, I hear. By the way, Pat Wentworth phoned and she is taking some of the children to the beach and if you go now and join her, she will be on the beach in back of the bank building, looking for you."

Jill hurried into her swim suit and ran down Cleaves Street, across Main Street and alongside the bank building, down the beach. The children hailed her with glad screams and ran to the water's edge with Pat after them. It seemed to Jill that everybody on the beach shouted with well-being and happiness. She plunged in and squealed. "Oh, the water's cold!" She swam to the raft.

"Hi!" someone greeted her, and she looked up to see Tommy Andrews grinning and holding out a hand to her. She did not take it, but she bounced out of the water and sat on the edge of the raft. She was glad to see Tommy and she wished she had taken his helping hand, but she had suddenly felt bashful again.

Then Tommy challenged her to a race to shore and Jill agreed happily. Both dived at the same time. Tommy had more speed than Jill and came in first.

"Say," he greeted her, "you're good, Jill."

Pat came running toward them. "You're good, Jill," she added her praise. Other girls and boys joined them and they all sunned and dried themselves on the sand. Pat had to leave with her young sister and brothers. She whispered to Jill, "I hope I get a letter from Mr. Putnam. I wish so much for that iron-gray horse that he advertised."

"Let me know if you get a letter," Jill whispered back.

Four days went by and no letter came. Then Pat phoned Jill.

"You have to come to the rescue. The girl who takes a part in Jo March's play has a fever and her mother is keeping her in bed. The play is tomorrow afternoon."

"What do you mean? What are you talking about?" Jill asked.

Pat tried to explain. "The Girl Scouts are putting on a play, *Little Women*. You have read the book by Louisa Alcott, haven't you?"

Jill said, yes, of course, she knew the story of *Little Women*.

"The last rehearsal is today and you must go with me. I promised Mrs. Norton you would help out," Pat declared firmly.

There was a stunned silence. Jill was so startled she couldn't speak and she could hardly swallow. She was panic-stricken. "I—I can't."

Pat pleaded, "Jill, you must help out. It is a tiny part and you are so smart you can learn the few words. I'll come and get you right away. We must hurry." Pat hung up.

Jill moved in a daze all the way to the small Finnish Temperance Hall on Forest Street where they joined other girls running up a flight of steps. Jill saw the stage filled with costumed girls milling around. She was told to sit in the front row until called. Her eyes roved around, noting the flowered curtains blowing at the opened windows. On the walls were large framed photographs of dour-looking men with drooping mustaches. The back of the stage had a painted drop depicting a sweep of ocean with a rising sun and a rainbow.

The curtain was lowered, and she heard a child near her exclaim, "It's just like a real curtain." The painted green draperies had gold-painted tassels and fringes. The curtain was yanked up again.

Pat came to her. She was dressed as a boy. "I'm Laurie," she said. "You watch now, we're going to begin. The first scene is in the March's home in December, 1863. You don't come until the second scene in Act One. Mrs. Norton will call you in time."

Jill was petrified. Whatever happened in the first scene made no impression on her. She shivered and trembled with fear when the curtain came down. In a jiffy, Pat was pushing her backstage.

Mrs. Norton said, "Between the scenes, some of the girls sing, so let me rehearse you now. This is

57

Jo's playlet 'The Witch's Curse.' It shows an imprisoned maiden in a tower."

Jill gasped with surprise. The tower was a huge carton painted like a stone tower. A cut-out window, a few feet from the floor, showed a girl's head wearing a coronet. The girl stood on a bucket inside the tower.

Trina Jensen, who took the part of Roderigo, the lover, swaggered on, singing a sentimental love song. She knelt at the foot of the tower, pleading with the imprisoned maiden to marry him. The girl in the tower declared she would leap from the tower rather than marry her father's choice. "If I cannot marry you, my handsome, dashing Roderigo, I shall enter a convent for I shall never marry another."

Roderigo begged her to step down from the tower, and flee with him. A box was brought hastily to the foot of the tower for the maiden to step on. She started to climb through the window.

At this point, Jill was to shout in a loud, masculine voice, "Zara! Zara! Whither dost thou go?"

Jill was Don Pedro, the cruel father of Zara.

Zara screamed, "Quick! My father! We are discovered!"

Jill, as Don Pedro, appeared too late. The lover, Roderigo, and Zara fled from him.

Jill saw that she was not an important character,

and in spite of her timidity, the playlet went off without a hitch. "You'll have a costume ready tomorrow," Mrs. Norton told her.

The confusion of squealing, giggling girls and the singers practicing in one part of the hall put Jill in such a state of dismay that she could hardly wait to get away from it all.

"Pat," she moaned on the way home. "I can't do it—I'm too frightened and I think I'm going to cry."

Pat flashed out. "Don't act like a baby, Jill Stewart. Maybe some of the others are scared too, but that doesn't keep them from doing their duty as Girl Scouts."

"But I'm not a Girl Scout," Jill blubbered.

"Heck!" Pat was angry. "Go on then and be a selfish pig."

Jill gulped. It hurt to have Pat call her a selfish pig and a crybaby. She whispered between sobs, "I'll try, I really will try."

Pat scowled at her woebegone face. "You just better try, or I won't be friends with you."

That threat was enough to make Jill stop sobbing. The rest of the walk home was quiet. Jill said good-by and promised to be at the hall, Saturday afternoon, in plenty of time to get dressed in her costume and be made up.

Saturday afternoon, when Jill saw the audience

beginning to come into the hall, she felt like someone in a bad dream. She was dressed in a costume and her face was made up. A glance in the mirror showed a face she had never seen before. Her brown eyes were larger, her cheeks were red, but they were almost covered with a beard and a mustache was pasted over a large, red mouth.

The play began. Trina Jensen, who played the part of Jo March, dominated the scene with her spirited performance. The first scene was over. Seven girls sang old-time songs for fifteen minutes. The second scene was ready and the curtain jerked up.

Jo March's play, "The Witch's Curse," took place in the family living room. The imprisoned maiden, Zara, was in the tower. Jill heard the dramatic dialogue between Zara and Roderigo. Now was the time for Jill, as Don Pedro the father, to rush toward the tower to prevent the lovers from eloping. She got caught on the tower, screamed wildly, and grabbed the edge of the cut-out window. The tower fell forward with the scenery on top of her, Zara, and Roderigo.

Pat, as Laurie began to laugh. Jo tried to rescue the play and she got up from the debris and shouted, "Be quiet, you bad boy, or you can go home."

Mrs. Norton, out of sight, hissed a warning. The real play got going again when the March girls, Amy,

Beth, Meg, and Jo received a telegram telling them their father had been wounded in the war.

The curtain shuddered down. Jill tore off her costume and found a door leading out of the hall. She was close to the back of a grocery store. She sat on a box letting the tears run down her face. She wept bitterly. She had failed Pat and she had made a mess of things. From the open windows of the hall she heard the high, sweet voice of Jo March. That was Trina Jensen, the tall blond girl who loved acting. Then the applause crashed through the windows. The play, *Little Women,* was over.

Jill slipped between the buildings and ran home as fast as she could. Never again would she act in a play or get up before an audience. She was a complete flop. Dashing in the front door, Jill flew upstairs to the bathroom to scrub her face clean of the make-up.

In a few minutes Aunt Emma came up with a freshly ironed dress of her own.

"I'm wearing this to church tomorrow," she said. Then she went on, "You are to go to choir rehearsal Tuesday at seven. I told the choirmaster that you'd sing in the choir and he was pleased."

Jill stood silent for an instant. Then a flash of temper shook her so that she stamped her feet and screamed, "I won't. I won't. I hate you!"

Aunt Emma was so dumfounded that she sat down and simply looked at Jill with wide-open eyes and open mouth. She could not seem to speak.

Jill was instantly sorry. She was amazed at herself. Never had she screamed at her parents. Never had she stamped her feet in anger. She was crushed. Aunt Emma slowly regained her usual poise.

"Virgilia Stewart. Go in your room and shut the door and don't come out until you are ready to apologize to me."

Aunt Emma's stern orders were obeyed. Jill sat in her room and thought about her disastrous experience as an actress. Her heart ached because she was sure she had lost Pat's friendship. She was ashamed of her outburst of temper. She did not hate Aunt Emma, in fact, she was growing fond of her.

With a sober face and shy air, she went downstairs to find Aunt Emma. "I'm sorry I was rude to you." She offered her apology in a subdued voice. "Please forgive me." Then she told Aunt Emma of her failure in the play and how clumsy she had been.

Aunt Emma said she would forgive her and not force her to sing in the choir. They ate supper and watched television and went to bed early. Jill felt sad. Her private wish to have a best friend would never come true. Pat did not admire her enough to have her as a best friend.

Chapter Five

Jill waited several days before she had the courage to face Pat. She had avoided being home when the Gloucester *Daily Times* was delivered. Finally, she had to see Pat no matter what the outcome might be. She sat on the front steps. Pat was coming up the lane.

"Hi!" she called in her usual cheerful voice. "Guess what?"

Jill said, "What? Tell me." She began to feel warm around her heart because Pat did not seem to be mad at her.

Pat announced, "I've got to hurry . . . but I had a letter from Mr. Putnam."

"Oh!" Jill cried. "What did he write?"

"He said that the horse was sold in a few days but he appreciated my interest and if he ever knew anyone with a horse for sale he would tell him to put an ad in the paper . . . and I'll have to watch the paper every day." Pat grinned with joy at the prospect of another horse for sale.

"I will watch too," Jill promised.

Pat was shoving the heavy doll buggy up the lane. She called back, "Ask your Aunt Emma to buy tickets from my mother for the Boiled Dinner, will you?"

Jill was eager to please Pat who had not mentioned a word about Jill's disgraceful acting in the play, *Little Women.* "I will," she called out.

It wasn't easy to persuade Aunt Emma to buy tickets for the Boiled Dinner the next Thursday evening. "Boiled Dinner is New England to be sure, but I don't hold with the way those women in the Universalist Church cook it. They like a flat piece of brisket of beef with lots of fat, and I don't. I want a solid, meaty piece of beef," Aunt Emma said firmly, then she weakened and added, "Oh, well, I'll phone Pat's mother that I'll take two tickets."

Aunt Emma had been shopping and was full of news about two men from out of town who were going around to old houses owned by widows or single women. "They tell them the chimneys need cleaning and they strike a reasonable bargain. But mind you, Jill, they start the work and then come in with a list of repairs that must be made or the house

66

will catch fire, and before the women know it, they are caught up in a big debt. Those men are swindlers. No repairs were needed and several poor, foolish women have signed papers ordering them to do the work."

Jill wasn't interested in chimney cleaners but Aunt Emma went on to say, "The police want to catch them. If they ever come to this house, I'll be ready and I'll call the police."

Jill murmured, "I'm going to the library now. My book is due today." She left Aunt Emma muttering to herself about what she'd do if those swindlers dared to come to her house.

Jill walked down Cleaves Street and stopped to say hello to Lucy Applebird.

"Come in and visit," she invited Jill. They sat in the living room and Lucy was her usual talkative self. Jill told her that she was going to a Boiled Dinner at the Universalist parish rooms.

"I wouldn't give a Hannah Cook for a boiled dinner," Lucy sputtered. She was interrupted by two men in the store. Jill heard them talk about the chimneys on the house and how crooked they were and dangerous. They pushed their way into the living room, and Lucy had to listen. "We'll clean the chimneys reasonably," one said. The other shook his head woefully, saying the chimneys must be dangerously crooked and ought to be rebuilt. Jill thought he had a bold, forceful manner. She was surprised when Lucy did not object. They were very insistent, and Lucy seemed almost under a spell, Jill thought.

Lucy Applebird seemed to agree with the man and said, "Well, it has been a long time since they were cleaned. You'll do a good job?"

"Sure, lady. And in a jiffy. You two ladies just sit down and take it easy," the first man said.

Lucy Applebird laughed. "Oh, I always take it easy."

"That's what keeps you so young looking," the second man winked at her. "Now show us where the cellar steps are so we can find where the chimneys start."

Jill was frightened. She remembered what Aunt Emma had said and realized that they might make Lucy sign an order for a big job that was not needed. She took a deep breath and made up her mind. She tiptoed to the rough room and ran lightly down the steps. Her heart was beating. She was sure the men would not let her out of the house, but she was determined to save Lucy from the swindlers.

Jill ran like mad between the Methodist Church and Town Hall, across Broadway, paying no attention to the angry drivers who tooted at her. She opened the wide door of the police station and

68

gasped to the policeman sitting behind the high desk. "Hurry and catch those swindlers. They are in Lucy Applebird's house."

"What swindlers?" The officer was alert. She stuttered, "The—the—chimney cleaners. They will cheat Lucy and they will say her chimneys need repairs and make her sign a paper."

She was out of breath. The officer was speaking through a microphone giving Lucy Applebird's address and all the information Jill had supplied.

She turned to go out. "Wait, girl. Tell me your name. I have to write this down." He smiled at her.

She gave him her name and where she lived.

"You're scared, my girl. You'd better sit down and wait until I hear from the officers in the prowl car." The policeman was friendly.

It wasn't long before the policeman told her she could go back to the Applebird house. "They have taken the men into custody, thanks to you," he said.

Jill went back, and Lucy Applebird hugged her. "Single women are foolish sometimes," she confessed. "A man around the house is a protection. Papa would never have been taken in by crooks. You tell your Aunt Emma what a brave girl you are, and here is your library book, don't forget it."

"Oh, it was nothing," Jill said modestly. She was still in a daze, wondering how she had ever had the

69

courage to make up her mind quickly and act, in spite of being scared.

Jill was unprepared for the newspaper account of her quick thinking and bravery. The swindlers had been in Gloucester and in Essex too, but no one had actually caught them at their tricks until now.

Later, when Pat came with the papers, she said, "I'm sorry I called you a crybaby and a selfish pig. You are brave. I would have been frightened to pieces. Supposing they had seen you running to the police station and had caught you and tortured you to make you keep quiet."

Jill giggled. Now that it was over, she thought it was not such a hard thing to do. She forgot how miserable she had been about the play, and she was happy to have Pat admire and praise her.

Pat started to continue her paper route. "I'll meet you at the Boiled Dinner, our whole family will be there, except for the twins."

At a quarter to six Jill and Aunt Emma stepped into the parish room of the Universalist Church. The long tables were set close together. Friends beckoned to Aunt Emma to sit beside them. There was a loud clamor of voices until the minister and his family came in. He tapped a fork against a glass and an instant hush fell on the waiting people while he asked a blessing on the meal.

Then a terrific bustle began. Bowls of mashed turnips and mashed squash were passed. Jill did what Aunt Emma did. This dinner was a new experience for her. She took a dab of each. Then platters of sliced cold corn beef, pats of butter, and baskets of rolls went up and down the tables. Jill took some of each. She looked up with surprise to see more food.

Several portly women came from the kitchen bearing aloft great platters piled high with wedges of grayish boiled cabbage in the center, with new boiled beets and baby carrots and ivory-colored boiled potatoes on the border.

Jill was amazed to see some people pour vinegar on their vegetables. A contented murmur filled the room and men, women, and children began to eat.

"Virgilia." Aunt Emma nudged her. "Eat the vegetables at least. The meat is too fat and greasy to suit me."

Jill was trying to separate bits of lean meat from the streaks of fat, with little success. It was all so strange she hardly knew what she thought of the meal. She refused coffee when cups were filled from huge pitchers.

"Hi!" said their waitress.

Jill looked up. It was Pat's mother. "You don't have much of an appetite, Jill," she remarked.

72

Aunt Emma snorted softly. "Humph, she won't starve."

The feast was topped off with apple pie made from the first green apples. Jill ate hers with pleasure. Finally, the dinner was over and people shook hands and chatted. Pat dashed up to Jill. "I'm stuffed to the gills," she laughed, "aren't you?"

"No," Jill admitted. "I'm not, but I'm not exactly empty." She and Pat giggled.

Aunt Emma brought some friends to the girls. "This is Virgilia Stewart who is staying with me for a year." The older people asked Jill questions about her brave deed in going to the police when the swindlers were at the Applebird house. Boys hung around the edge of the group eying her with sober respect. Pat grinned and hugged her. "I'm proud of Jill," she chirped.

Everybody started home. Jill yawned. She was beginning to feel like a New Englander and she listened politely when Aunt Emma gossiped and chattered all the way home. She decided it was interesting to know about Rockport doings and Rockport people. She had no such interests at home.

Every day Jill pored over the ads in the Gloucester *Daily Times*. Aunt Emma noticed her interest. "What are you looking for? Something special?"

"No," Jill said. She would not tell anybody about

73

Pat's wish for a horse and that she was looking for an ad telling of a horse for sale.

"I read the ads people put in the paper to find homes for kittens. Listen to this one: 'A home for two adorable black kittens. Housebroken. Acrobatic, gay, and entertaining. Must go together. Tel. Rockport 3570.'"

"There is one in the lost column. 'My fat black cat has double white paws, also white breast. Answers to Ursula. Rocky Neck. Call Danny, 4344.'"

Jill said, "I hope that cat is found. Listen to this one: 'Hitching kitten, female, gray and white. Last seen on Monday perched on chassis of car on ride to Main Street. Tel. 1517M.'"

Jill looked dreamy. She thought it would be fun to have a cat, one with double paws. Her cat would learn to wait for Charlie Nelson's fish truck. Her cat would have a tail not like tailless Polly, cousin Mary's cat. Her cat would be named . . ."

"Virgilia." Aunt Emma's voice was sharp with suspicion. "Don't get a notion in your head to have a cat. I can't stand them."

Jill put down the paper. It was useless to go on with the subject when Aunt Emma's face wore a locked-tight expression.

"I'm going to write to my father and mother." She went upstairs wondering what they might find interesting. She had described Lucy Applebird's house that artists sketched, knowing her mother's interest in painting. Now she would write to them about penny candy: "There are long strings of black licorice and I don't care for them but I have tasted yellow 'chicken corn,' and 'watermelon slices' filled with real-looking black seeds, and I like chocolate-brown 'baked beans.' I like the hearts with mottoes on them. Maybe you remember the mottoes, GOOD LUCK, HELLO BABY, and other silly words."

Jill put down her pen. She did not know what else to write that would interest her parents. She realized that her activities in Rockport had very little in common with her parents' lives. Their letters were fascinating and Jill read them over again, especially the letter from London telling about their visit to Madame Tussaud's waxworks:

"We were quite taken with the tableaus of famous leaders and victims of the French Revolution. The murder of the little princes in the Tower of London was enough to give us the chills. The fairy tale of Cinderella was very artistic. There were groups of our Presidents and also European royalty, gowned splendidly, and extremely lifelike. There were guards in natural positions, so real I could hardly believe my eyes."

Jill mused. "They must be awfully lifelike. I can't imagine how anyone can make such real-looking people out of wax."

She was aware of a rising wind blowing her curtains out straight. She shut the windows and went downstairs. Aunt Emma was at the phone. She turned to Jill. "Yes, of course she can tend the store for you, Lucy. You go right along and enjoy that funeral."

Jill was horrified. Did people enjoy funerals? Aunt Emma finished her conversation. Then she told Jill that Lucy Applebird's second cousin, Hosea Tarr, had died. He was ninety-nine years old.

"No one is sorry and no one is going to grieve for him. He was a helpless invalid, Virgilia. Lucy just called from a neighbor's phone. She does not have a phone. All the Tarr relatives will have a nice visit and talk about old times and sit down to a good meal, maybe for the last family get-together for some of them. They will put aside old quarrels and angers for the time being."

She had promised that Jill could go down to the store first thing in the morning.

She was reluctant to accept the responsibility, but Aunt Emma said, "Pooh, only kids will be coming in to buy candy. If anybody wants a box of crackers or cookies, I hope you have enough gumption to sell them without having cat fits."

Jill was meek after Aunt Emma's scolding.

Aunt Emma tuned in her kitchen radio set for the late weather report. The announcer had news of a hurricane on the Florida coast. "It will probably blow out to sea," said Aunt Emma. "We will get extra high tides and some wind, but nothing serious."

Chapter Six

Jill was up early. She didn't know whether she was looking forward to keeping the store or if she did not want to accept the responsibility. She had to make up her mind. Her mother and father were not there to advise her. Either she had to sell candy, cookies, and crackers or she had to say she was too shy to stand behind the counter and talk with strangers.

Aunt Emma put her lunch in a basket. "I gave you an apple turnover, some cold meat sandwiches, and two hard-boiled eggs. I guess that will keep you from starving, heh, heh." Jill tried to smile, but failed. Aunt Emma's jokes were few and far between. She looked so sober that Aunt Emma asked, "Why such a long face, don't you feel well?"

Jill was quick to say she felt fine. She really felt sickish.

"Maybe it's this unsettled weather," Aunt Emma suggested.

Jill had a feeling of apprehension that seemed to settle in her stomach. "There is nothing to be afraid of," she told herself. She went out the door. "Good-by," she called back to Aunt Emma.

Jill got the key from Mrs. Riley across the street from the store. She went in and pulled back the faded cretonne curtains that hung in the store windows at night. She looked into the rough room and saw the flag hanging listlessly on the flagpole.

"Lucy Applebird was up very early," Jill said to herself.

She found the living room orderly. The cot bed where Lucy slept was made up, and the canary hopped around in his clean cage, but he did not sing.

Then the bell on the store door jingled and two small boys came in with a few pennies to spend. They leaned hard against the curved glass front, pointing at the varieties of candy.

"Don't press on the glass front, you'll break it," Jill imitated Lucy Applebird. One boy made an impudent face at her. They haggled over their choices. At last, well satisfied with their penny candy, they left, banging the door behind them, and enjoying the violent jingling of the bell.

A woman came in demanding a loaf of bread.

"We don't have bread to sell," Jill told her.

"But you used to. I always bought it here. I live in a summer cottage down the street. When did Lucy stop selling bread?" The woman was annoyed.

Jill told her that Lucy Applebird would have to buy large quantities of bread from the delivery trucks. "She couldn't sell so much bread," Jill explained.

The woman decided to take a box of common crackers and a box of vanilla wafers. "Where is Lucy?" the woman asked.

"She went to a funeral in Gloucester and will be gone all day," Jill said. She remembered the swindlers who cleaned chimneys and she was frightened to think she would be alone all day.

The customer left and from then on Jill's trade was mostly with children. She ate some of her lunch. The wind began to blow harder and the sky turned a dark, heavy gray. Jill talked to the canary huddled on its perch. She looked at the brightly colored pictures on the many calendars. She read the old greeting cards. She watered the plants in the windows and the hours dragged along. At last a customer came in the store and Jill ran to wait on him. To her surprise it was Tommy Andrews.

"Jill," he said. "You must go home right away. The radio says the hurricane is due to hit the coast. Any minute now." He was breathless from running. "Didn't you hear the wind?"

"How did you know I was here?" she questioned.

"Your Aunt Emma phoned my mother to ask if I'd get you home."

"But I must stay here and take care of the store," Jill faltered. She felt responsible for the store. Lucy had trusted her and no matter what happened she was not going to run home. The wind was rising and howling. Rain streaked the windows and they rattled and shook with the blast of the rising hurricane. Jill had never heard such noise. The store door blew open and Tommy thrust himself against it and forced it shut while Jill turned the key to lock it.

"We must shut the windows," Tommy cried. He ran to the rough room. The door to the porch was open and banging and a window blew in, and Jill heard the splintering glass fall into the room. Tommy pushed her out of the room, luckily neither were hit by flying glass.

"You go through the house . . . I'll have to board up this window, somehow." Tommy's face was wet from rain. He fumbled around for loose pieces of lumber.

Jill ran to the living room and shut the windows. The plants were all on the floor with broken pots and scattered leaves. Rain was pouring in. She saw a huge elm come crashing down near Town Hall, it just escaped the back of the Methodist Church, but it covered several cars parked there. The sound of trees cracking and crashing came from another direction. She ran to the little front hall. A tree was lying against the house. She could see it through the narrow panes of glass at each side of the front door.

Under the door leading upstairs, a trickle of water was spreading rapidly over the floor. She opened the door and went up the wet steps. She could not see where the water came from. The two upper rooms were dry. Then she saw, from under a wall, a flood of rain bubbling out on the floor toward the stairway. She put her hands on the wall and to her surprise it was movable, although it was papered like the rest of the room. She stared. "This must be a door. I'll have to open it because the water is coming from some place higher up." She was frantic. It was no use yelling for Tommy to help her, he would never hear her in the howling rage of the hurricane.

She felt around and found a hole. She put in two fingers and pulled. The door opened on a most unusual flight of steps down which the rain was running in a flood.

Jill was frightened. But she knew she had to do her best to save Lucy's rooms. Her feet took her up. Instead of a step built as usual, each step was cut in two; one foot rested on half of a step while she moved the other foot to the next half step. A rope looped from top to bottom helped her up the steep little steps. She stumbled into a rough, small room like an attic. Above her, a deeply framed square of glass on a long iron rod was banging up and down. She tried to reach the rod to pull it shut, but she did not have the strength.

"I need a chair to stand on." She went down the wet steps and found a small chair. She was about to push it up the queer steps when a strong gale ripped the scuttle off and it crashed with a splintering of glass. Shingles blew off and the roof was opened to the driving rain. Jill stood in a daze. Then she clambered up the steps, half-realizing that she was in the mysterious room she had wondered and dreamed about. From outside she had not seen the old-fashioned glass scuttle on the flat roof that let in light and air.

There was a table with a photograph on it, showing a pretty girl smiling into the face of a handsome young man with large, dark eyes and black, curly hair. The rain drove against Jill's face, but still she stared. There was a hat wreathed with flowers, hanging on a nail and beside it a dress, all ruffles and flounces and ribbons, dangling in the rain. Jill's hair hung over her eyes. She pushed it back and looked

at a china box, painted all over with flowers, on the table. Inside, there was a yellowed newspaper clipping in fine print. She could not read it and she closed the lid quickly. She knew she had stumbled on a secret. "I must save these things for Lucy," she muttered.

Jill reached for the dress and the hat and the photograph. A blast of wind snatched the dress and hat from her wet hand and blew them through the ragged holes of the roof. The dress caught on a snag and in a moment it was in tatters. The hat was a soggy lump that went sailing off in the wind and rain. Jill was hit on her arm by a flying shingle.

Somehow she managed to stumble down the steps into a bedroom. She heard a crash from the front yard, and through the rain-streaked window she saw that the old flagpole was down. The torn flag went through the air and dropped into a corner of the yard.

"Jill! Where are you?" She could not answer Tommy's panicky cry. She seemed to be coming out of a daze. In one hand she held a faded, wet photograph. "Where did I get this?" She could not remember snatching it up. She had a feeling that she must hide it from Tommy. This photograph was important to Lucy Applebird. She thrust it in a bureau drawer under the pile of towels. Tommy burst in. His face and hands were grimy and his clothes sopping wet.

"Gee, I was worried about you, Jill. When I heard the noise up here and saw the shingles flying off the roof—what happened? You look sick."

Jill struggled to speak. "I'm all right. I was trying to pull down a scuttle in that room without a window, but I couldn't—the wind was too strong."

Tommy gasped, "You could have been hurt. Look, your arm is bleeding."

"A shingle blew against me," Jill said. "It's nothing."

They eyed each other. Jill thought Tommy looked like a scarecrow. She took a step, and the water squished in her rain-soaked shoes. The canary was trying to sleep, the room was so dark. Tommy tried a light. "The wires are down, no electricity. I guess there has been a lot of damage."

"It is getting lighter," Jill muttered. She was cold and wet. "There isn't so much noise now."

Tommy threw himself in a chair. "I got that window in the rough room boarded up with some old lumber. I found rusty nails and a hammer that haven't been used for years. I bet they belonged to old Mr. Applebird."

Jill flopped on the cot bed. "Will Lucy get back tonight? Would her relatives let her come back? I'd hate to have her see this mess. All her plants are broken and the flagpole is down."

Tommy shook his head. "Nobody is going out in a car tonight. The buses won't run. You see, the roads must be blocked with fallen trees. You come along now and go home."

"But what will happen to this house with that roof on the little room all full of holes?" she said worriedly.

Tommy consoled her. "Every carpenter and handy man will be busy boarding up windows and repairing roofs. The rain has stopped. Come on."

They stepped out. Cleaves Street was littered with wet leaves and branches and shingles. There was a hoarse, angry roar from the beach. "The tide is going to be high. I'm glad I don't live on Bearskin Neck. The waves wash across it from one side to the other side," Tommy said.

They picked their way up the dismal street. Dishwater Lane had runnels of rain pouring down in deep ruts. Tommy left Jill at the bottom of the hill. "Be seeing you," he called. They had to grin because each looked so bedraggled, dirty, and wet. Jill plodded up the hill.

Aunt Emma had lighted an ancient kerosene lamp in the kitchen. "Land's sake, you look like a drowned rat," she cried. "You poor girl." Aunt Emma opened

88

her arms and took the wet, shivering girl into her warm embrace. In no time she had Jill in a hot bath.

"Might as well use the hot water while we have it. With deliveries of fuel oil off for a few days, we may not have hot water enough to fill the tub."

Jill's arm was bandaged, and she dried her hair in front of the wood-burning kitchen stove. Hot milk relaxed her tense muscles. Aunt Emma chattered about how little damage had been done around the house. "Too bad the half-grown pears were blown down. There will be no canning pears this fall, but I have a few jars left from last year, down cellar. I'll miss the crab-apple jelly I always make."

Jill looked out at the crab-apple tree that rested its branches on the low kitchen roof. The small yellow apples that had laid their rosy cheeks on the old gray shingles were scattered over the grass.

"I could pick up some for you," Jill offered.

"Thank you." Aunt Emma smiled. "You are taking an interest in housekeeping I see." Then she went on, "That funeral in Gloucester would have had to be postponed and so Lucy will be away a few days longer than she expected. I hope her roof is repaired before she comes back and sees how much damage was done to it."

Jill yawned. The kitchen rocker was padded with

a ruffled seat and a soft back. They had eaten supper.
"Up to bed you go, Virgilia."

Aunt Emma was firm. She tucked Jill in, and gave
her a loving pat when she said good night. Jill was
too tired to think about her terrifying adventure and
Lucy Applebird's secret room and its mystery. That
would wait for another day.

Chapter Seven

The next days were cleaning-up days. So many trees had blown down that the town's street department worked overtime hauling them away to the dump or off the roads. Men from the electric company climbed poles to restore service in the town. Telephone men climbed poles too, repairing broken lines. Jill was hoping the Applebird house would be fixed up before Lucy managed to get away from her relatives and the postponed funeral. Otherwise it wouldn't be a happy homecoming.

Lucy Applebird came back before the roof was repaired. "I want those men to fix it the way it was long ago," she told Jill. She had a haunted look and she gave Jill a queer smile, then led her into the living room to hear the story of the hurricane without any details omitted.

Jill tried to avoid telling what she had seen in the tower room. But Lucy prodded her and questioned her and finally said, "Jill, I'm not going to beat around the bush any longer. I know what you found and I will tell you about it. You were a brave girl to stay here and try to take care of things."

Then Lucy began: "Long ago I worked in Gloucester in a millinery store. I was about eighteen then. One day I met a young fisherman coming up from the wharf. He had a big haddock by the gills. Somehow it slipped from his hand and I laughed. It fell at my feet and I almost stepped on its wet, slippery tail. He held out a hand to keep me from going down."

Lucy was silent, and Jill could almost see those young people looking into each other's eyes, laughing and still holding hands.

"That was just the beginning," Lucy went on. "We met whenever he was in port. Then my father heard about us from a relative, Hosea Tarr, who was buried the other day. Tony was Italian and his religion was different from mine, and Papa, who was a real hard-shell Baptist, said I was not to see him again, ever."

Lucy Applebird's face had a faraway expression. She began again. "We were going to be married, we planned to run away—and I had a pretty dress and a sweet hat to wear. Tony was on a fishing trip, and when he came back we were going to New Hampshire for a secret marriage. But he did not come back. All hands were lost at sea in a storm."

Jill felt tears rolling down her cheeks. Lucy's story was so sad, sadder than any story she had ever read, and wept over.

Lucy said, "All I had was the newspaper report of his death, which I kept in a china box, and his photograph. There is no grave to visit, so all I can do is to go to Gloucester and drop flowers on the outgoing tide and say a prayer for him."

Jill's tears flowed freely. All Lucy's tokens of her long-ago romance were gone, torn away on the howling winds. Then she remembered. "I saved a photograph for you and I put it in a bureau drawer under a pile of towels."

"You did?" Lucy smiled wistfully. "Bless you, Jill. But I guess the time has come for me to destroy that, too. I wouldn't want anyone to find it when I'm gone. I'll burn it along with the rag that was my American flag. That is proper. I am a D.A.R., and I know burning is the thing to do with our sacred belongings."

Jill wiped the tears from her face. "What is a D.A.R.?"

Lucy was happy to tell her all about her ancestors who fought in the Revolutionary War and how, from generation to generation, the pride of such service

94

was kept alive by the organization known as the Daughters of the Revolution.

Then Lucy spoke briskly. "That was my secret. You are the only one to share it with me, and please keep it a secret between us."

Jill promised faithfully to keep it a secret forever. They were interrupted by a man in the store. "Hi, Miss Applebird, you home?"

Lucy rose from her rocking chair and went in the store. "I hear you want me to repair your roof." The man was dressed in carpenter's overalls. Jill joined them.

"I want the roof the way it was before Papa built that crazy room on top. It always leaked around the flashings, and that scuttle was a lot of trouble. The window in the rough room is blown out and my flagpole is down." She listed the things to be done.

"Yes'm. I'll do all that, but I can't put up that old flagpole, it's cracked down the whole length. Say, wasn't that an old mast?" he asked.

"Yup," Lucy told him. "It came from the *Annie Stewart*." She turned to Jill. "Well, I declare, that vessel belonged to your grandpa, James Stewart. It was a coastwise vessel hauling lumber down from Maine."

Jill's eyes opened in surprise. "I never heard about that. I thought he was a merchant."

"He was," Lucy told her. "But when this vessel was wrecked at Eastern Point, he gave up the sea and took to the dry land. The mast was salvaged along with some other parts of the ship. The wheelhouse was pulled up and used for a children's playhouse."

Jill left Lucy and her carpenter planning repairs.

Later on, when Jill saw Pat delivering the Gloucester *Daily Times,* she remembered that they were going to watch the advertising page to see if a horse was for sale. "Pat, did you read about any horses for sale?"

"No," Pat said. "But I will have to stop wishing for a horse, I guess." She looked so gloomy that Jill cried out, "Why? You have lots of money saved to buy a horse."

"No." Pat's voice was on the edge of breaking into sobs.

"I gave it to my father. We need a new roof on the kitchen ell, the storm tore off most of the shingles and a falling limb from a tree in the back yard made a hole at the edge of the roof."

Jill was indignant. "You didn't have to give up your savings, did you?"

Pat looked at Jill in surprise. "Of course I did. I belong to a family and we all work together to keep

96

our house nice and happy . . . only I don't feel so happy. I wish, I wish so much for a horse."

Jill thought about Pat's serious words. She hesitated to speak her mind, her usual shyness held her back from stating her opinion. Then she took a long breath and said, "Pat, wishing isn't enough. You have to DO something about your wish."

"Do something?" Pat was puzzled. "What do you mean?"

Jill was so surprised at herself that she hardly knew what she meant Pat should do.

"I'll have to give it some thought," she said, thinking her father would say something like that.

Pat waited. "Think hard, Jill."

"Isn't there some way to make a lot of money in a hurry?" Jill wondered. "How do people make money for a need or a project?"

Pat blinked her eyes. She tried to think what was done in Rockport. "They have a play or a dance or a church supper or a fair."

"I think we should do something real soon so you can buy a horse to ride this summer," Jill said. But that was as far as they got, because Aunt Emma came out and wanted the paper to read about the damage all around Cape Ann.

While Jill and Aunt Emma were eating, Jill questioned her about church suppers. She heard how much cooking and planning and selling of tickets went into a successful outcome. Dances were something about which Aunt Emma professed ignorance. Plays involved rehearsals, learning parts, and at that Jill remembered with shame her flop in the play, *Little Women.*

"Tell me about fairs," she went on.

Aunt Emma looked at her with a gleam in her eyes. "Virgilia, I believe you are getting the feeling of Rockport. It must be the Stewart blood coming out in you." With a satisfied look she proceeded to go into details about how a fair was handled.

"First, you need a large lawn for the various tables. One table would be for baked goods and another table for fancy work, aprons, and knitted things. You should have a table for old books and magazines, they attract summer visitors mostly. You ought to see the way used clothing is sold and old shoes and hats! I never contribute anything to those departments, because I wear out and use up all my clothes and hats and shoes. They are not fit for anything when I get through with them."

Aunt Emma went on thinking about fairs. "Oh yes —I hear that over in Annisquam they have a Punch-and-Judy show put on by a college professor in the village hall. Then there is the lady portrait painter who puts on a show called the waxworks. I have never seen it, so I can't tell you any more about it. Oh, yes, they have tea and cookies served under a tent beside the village hall. At night they have fireworks, and supper cooked and eaten outdoors. My lands, they make a couple thousand dollars."

Jill brooded on all Aunt Emma's descriptions. When she went upstairs to bed, she reread her mother's letter from London. An idea was beginning to grow in the back of her mind. She could hardly wait for tomorrow to talk with Pat.

In the morning Jill hurried to Pat's house to find a busy scene: men working on the kitchen roof, while the children picked up old shingles and piled them in the barn. Pat's mother was trying to get order in her kitchen where dust from the roof and rain from the storm had covered everything.

Jill helped Pat with the shingles. She looked around the barn with so much interest, poking into corners and exploring the hayloft, that Pat laughed at her. Jill confessed she had never been in a barn before. "I like this barn. It has great possibilities," she said.

Pat put down a pile of shingles. Her face and hands were smeared with dust. "Can't you stop and sit down awhile?" Jill asked. "I want to talk."

Pat heaved a sigh. "I'm ready to take a break." She sat down beside Jill, on a bench.

"I have an idea," Jill began. She was a little reluctant to bring out her ideas, but she had decided that in order to have her wish granted, to have a best friend, she would have to be a best friend herself. Pat's blue eyes were fixed on her.

"We can have a fair in the barn and in this yard and raise money to buy you a horse," Jill burst out.

Pat was too surprised to do anything but squeak like a startled mouse. Jill went on. "Aunt Emma told me about fairs and I'm sure she will help with some things that older people can do. But my idea is have a waxworks exhibition right here in the barn."

"What are you talking about?" Pat asked.

Jill had her mother's letter in her blouse pocket and she read it to Pat. Slowly, Pat began to understand and, slowly, she grew more and more enthusiastic.

Jill said, "If we can get someone to put make-up on the characters so that they look real, that would help."

Pat said, "An actress maybe? Oh, I know, Mrs. Norton who directed *Little Women* was an actress, she would help, I bet." Pat's eyes sparkled. "What about costumes? How about lighting effects and scenery?"

Jill asked, "Would your father help?"

"Sure," Pat nodded. "But you will have to think up the groups and what they represent, Jill. You know so much because you read a lot."

Jill admitted she had been thinking about that. "I'm making a list of groups that won't need costumes we can't possibly get."

Suddenly she bubbled over. "I've got the best idea! There is an old sleigh in Aunt Emma's yard nearly buried in tall grass. We could haul it up here. Now what do you think that could be used for?"

Pat was thoughtful. So was Jill. Pat ventured, "I think of Santa Claus, but we couldn't get reindeer ... how about 'Over the river and through the woods, to Grandfather's house we go . . .'" She sang it softly. "That's an old-fashioned Thanksgiving song."

"I like that," Jill said. "I was thinking of 'Jingle Bells,' but your idea is best and it would be easy to fix it up with a man driving and a family all bundled up in the sleigh ready to drive to Grandpa's on a cold day."

The girls were interrupted by the appearance of Tommy and his friend, Eric Jensen.

"Shall we tell them?" Pat whispered.

Jill thought fast. If they told the boys why they were going to have a fair, they would know about Pat's secret wish for a horse. "You'll have to, because we can't raise money under false pretenses."

"You are right. You tell them," Pat said.

The boys listened to Jill's plan for a fair and how it was to raise money for Pat to buy a horse. The boys stared at them.

"Are you crazy?" Tommy asked. "Do you know how much a horse costs?"

Pat said, "Of course. About a hundred and fifty dollars. One was advertised but I didn't have enough money saved up to buy it."

Jill explained, "She had over fifty dollars saved, but she gave it to her father. He didn't have enough to pay to fix the roof. He's buying a new used car."

103

Pat broke in, "Our old car wasn't large enough for all the family."

"Gee!" Tommy exclaimed. "Where would you have a fair?"

"Right here," Pat told him. "You listen to Jill's plans. They are good."

Chapter Eight

After several meetings of what Pat called the steering committee, consisting of the two girls, Tommy, and Eric Jensen and his sister Trina, they went to see Mrs. Norton. She was amused at first and then her interest grew. "It is a fine project to keep you busy, but you can't do all this just to buy a horse for Pat. If you want a good attendance you need something more general, more of public interest."

The girls eyed each other soberly. Jill spoke up. They could give some of the money to the D.A.R., she suggested. That made Mrs. Norton laugh. "They don't need money."

Pat had an idea. "How about the Girl Scouts? We are always trying to sell cookies and salted nuts to raise money."

Mrs. Norton beamed. "That is really splendid. The

Scouts will help to sell tickets to the waxworks. Oh, that's really splendid."

Jill and Pat grinned at each other. From then on plans went along fast and furious. Pat's father said he would arrange the lighting for the waxworks. Aunt Emma promised to enlist her friends to contribute to the baked goods. Lucy Applebird said she would help sell. She thought she might have some old-fashioned clothing tucked away that would do for costumes. "I hardly know what's stored away in my house," she said. Then she added, "I suppose I ought to get rid of my old coonskin coat, it is so bare in spots. Dogs bark at it. People snicker at it."

Jill had noticed that ever since the hurricane and the loss of the tower room, Lucy had not been her usual, brisk self. It seemed as if the memory of her romance, the dress, the hat, and photograph had kept her young when she could actually touch and see them. Now they were gone.

But the fair stimulated her. Not only did Lucy Applebird find old-fashioned clothes for some of the waxworks figures to wear, but she gathered together old schoolbooks covered with gingham that was sewed and laced on the inside covers. There were dolls with china heads and painted smiles unchanged through the years. They were dressed in hand-sewn clothes in a long-forgotten style.

Lucy also brought out an iron savings bank with a horse and rider that galloped when a penny was dropped in a slot. Pat took them away in her doll buggy when she finished delivering papers.

Hauling the old sleigh from Aunt Emma's back yard to the Wentworth barn was a problem. At last Tommy and his friends tied it on to two boys' wagons and somehow it made the trip without mishap. The real task was planning the waxworks to fit the limited space in the barn. Jill thought Trina would be a fine master of ceremonies, the one who would guide the spectators from group to group, giving a speech about each group and what it represented.

Jill wrote the speeches and rehearsals began. Mrs. Norton helped and encouraged them when they were tired and cranky, and wanted nothing so much as to quit and go swimming.

Mr. Wentworth experimented with lighting effects until he found bulbs of the right color to give the faces of the waxworks figures a real, lifelike glow. He arranged to be in the open hayloft where he could shine a spotlight on each group.

Joey, Elizabeth, and Paul were given parts. Aunt Emma's friends planned to bring their cakes and cookies and pies to the Wentworth back yard, which they began to call the fair grounds. All the older people were delighted to have their children busy and out of mischief.

Jill forgot to feel shy and frightened of doing things in front of people. She was writing furiously. Her speeches for the master of ceremonies were finished at last. And at last the day of the fair dawned bright and clear with an ocean breeze to cool the summer heat.

Before the fair was officially open, people began to come. The only advertising had been by word of mouth, but the local reporter was told about the fair and she was on hand to take pictures for the Gloucester *Daily Times*. She was famous for her photographs of children.

The waxworks were to be shown every half hour, and ten tickets were sold for each showing. Jill was in the first scene. Ten people, young and old, came into the barn. The wide doors were closed. It was dark inside and people coming in from the blazing sunshine could not see a thing. Trina wore white trousers, a dark jacket, and she had on an old high hat. A dark mustache covered her upper lip. She began, "Do not handle or touch the figures. It is a hot day and fingers may damage the delicate wax figures."

A spotlight flashed on two bathing beauties. "Here you see the change of style in bathing suits. Observe how the ladies in the Gay Nineties were covered up with bloomers, and skirts over the bloomers. Long black stockings and rubber sneakers were worn."

Pat and Jill held hands and stood in a walking position. They were motionless while the master of ceremonies went on:

"Observe the modern girl, free as a bird in her swim suit." Jill's hand shook a bit as the people stared at her and Pat did not dare to tighten her hold.

"Gee!" a small boy whispered. "They are not real people. They don't move. Mom, are they real?" He reached out a finger to jab Jill.

"Hush, come along." His mother dragged him to the next display.

The lights were now played on the sleigh. Trina began:

"Here, ladies and gentlemen, we have the famous picture, by Grandma Moses, of an old-fashioned country Thanksgiving."

The spectators stared at a father and mother in the front seat of a sleigh with a moth-eaten buffalo robe over their laps. The father pretended he had a pair of horses in front of him. He held his arms as if he were driving. His wife cuddled beside him. The children in the other seat were bundled up for cold weather. A close observer would have seen perspiration standing out on Papa's forehead. He was Joey, and Mama was Elizabeth. Paul and two friends made up the rest of the family.

Trina began to sing in her high, sweet voice the first verse of the song: "Over the river and through the woods,/To Grandmother's house we go./The horse knows the way to carry the sleigh,/Through the white and drifted snow."

Then the light was turned to the next group.

Red Ridinghood stood dressed all in red with a basket on her arm. She had a scared look as she half-turned her head backwards. Right behind her was an odd-looking wolf. It was a boy on his hands and feet wearing a coonskin coat. Even if he looked more like a rare animal than a wolf, it was very effective. From where Pat and Jill were located, still not moving, they saw the spectators go on to admire "The Spirit of '76." Jill thought the scene would please Lucy Applebird and other members of the D.A.R.

Tommy and two friends who played in the high school band had consented to be the soldiers, one with a drum and one with a fife. Tommy carried a flag and he wore a bloody bandage around his head. The master of ceremonies gave a short description of the painting they represented. "Hurrah!" a small boy yelled. He was thrilled with this scene.

"Moses in the Bulrushes," Trina announced. There,

among some rushes, kneeled a girl supposed to be dressed like Pharoah's daughter. She was reaching for a basket containing a life-size baby doll. The basket rested on a mirror that represented the river where the baby Moses was set adrift.

"My, isn't it stunning," Jill heard a lady say.

The last group was one figure in the horse stall. Little Bopeep with a toy lamb, stood with a crook in one hand. She was all pink and white, with golden hair, and the ladies purred, "Oh, how sweet!"

The light was turned off and the spectators went out, hugely satisfied with the waxworks, and each marveled, "How could they hold those poses so long?"

The visitors turned to the tables loaded with food for sale. Lucy Applebird did a lively business selling cakes and cookies and pies. She scolded one little girl who stuck a finger into a lemon-meringue pie. "Now I'll have to mark it down, you can't get full price for damaged goods," she sputtered.

The hubbub grew. The reporter took pictures. The summer visitors bought the old schoolbooks, babbling with delight to find some valuable *McGuffey's Readers*. The dolls brought high prices, for Pat's mother knew they were worth a good deal of money. The old iron bank was bought by a collector of iron banks.

In the barn the waxworks characters relaxed. They would repeat their performance in half an hour.

"Jill, isn't this fun?" Pat cried. Jill agreed. She was having fun and it didn't bother her to have the spectators stare at her. Mrs. Norton said she was thrilled. She went around renewing make-up where it was needed. The second showing went on. This time Jill felt at ease and her hand didn't tremble. Trina was in her element. Eric said she was "hamming it up." Trina giggled. She loved acting. Her mustache wobbled and Mrs. Norton renewed the glue that held it. The waxworks was shown four times.

Aunt Emma said later that she never had seen kids drink so much lemonade. The homemade candy was sold out in a jiffy.

"We could have sold more baked goods, the summer folks are wild about home cooking. When they live in small cottages and don't want to spend time cooking they watch for every sale of home-baked goods." She was proud of the sales.

Aunt Emma asked Pat's mother, "How much did we take in?"

"I'm not sure, Mr. Norton has charge of the money. Didn't his little Debbie make the prettiest Bopeep you ever saw?"

They talked and talked about the whole afternoon. Jill and Pat helped to clean up the barn. The boys took back all the borrowed clothes, tables, and stage properties, except the sleigh. The girls were too busy and happy to give any thought to the profits earned by the fair.

At last it was time to go home. Jill saw Mr. Norton come out of Pat's house. "Girls," he said, "don't you want to know how much money you took in?"

They looked at each other and giggled. "I guess we forgot about that." They said it together and that made them giggle harder than ever.

"Well, I have here one hundred and fifty dollars and sixty cents." He shook the box of money.

The girls stared at each other. Jill spoke first. "Your half of that should be enough for a horse, Pat, and, oh boy, the Girl Scouts should be pleased with their share."

Pat could not say a word. Then she stammered, "A horse . . . a horse of my own . . . a horse. Oh, Jill, you made my wish come true. Jill, you are my best friend."

At those words Jill knew her own secret wish to have a best friend had come true. It was so wonderful that she forgot her shyness and impulsively hugged Pat.

"Oh, thank you, Pat, you are my best friend too." They looked so happy that Mr. Norton laughed. "Come girls, you deserve to have your wishes. This is quite an undertaking for you youngsters to have put over."

Jill rose to go home. "We must watch the ads in the Gloucester *Times,* don't forget, Pat."

"I won't!" Pat's joyful voice rang out. Jill went along. "Be seeing you," she called back.

Chapter Nine

Day after day Jill and Pat scanned the page of ads in the Gloucester *Daily Times*. There were fascinating ads about kittens and even elderly cats in need of adoption. Now and then a puppy would be offered free, but there was no ad telling of a horse for sale.

In the meantime the people in Town Hall missed seeing Lucy Applebird's flag from their office windows, and a plan was made to supply a flagpole of metal that would stand the stress and strain of coastal storms. A celebration was arranged for the presentation of a new flag with fifty stars.

Lucy was told about it and the members of the D.A.R. were asked to be present. Jill was almost as pleased as Lucy, and she said she would be there. "My best friend and I will watch the ceremony," she said.

Lucy beamed. "Jill, you are learning to smile. I declare when I first saw you I wondered if you knew how to smile. A smile is very becoming to you, in fact a smile looks good on anyone, no matter how plain and homely they are."

Jill smiled and looked pleased. She wasn't used to compliments.

"I want all the children who buy penny candy to be there too. They must join in singing 'The Star-Spangled Banner.' I'm to sing the first verse alone."

Pat was all agog when Jill told her about the celebration.

"I hope it is a nice day so I can wear the new dress my mother made me for the first day of school. It's plaid."

"School?" Jill was surprised. She had forgotten that the summer was passing and in a few weeks she would start to a new school. For a moment she felt a shrinking away from an experience that would bring her in contact with new teachers and unknown girls and boys.

"Oh, dear," she sighed, and her face grew long.

"Jill, don't be scared. I'll be with you to show you our school and teachers." Jill smiled a little. The smile made her feel less scared. It was such fun to have a helpful and understanding best friend.

119

The day of the ceremony was rainy and cold. Jill and Pat, wearing raincoats, stood inside the ragged yard beside the tottering old shed on the road. This was where Jill had first spied Lucy Applebird raising her flag and singing. People gathered under umbrellas. The rain turned to a foggy drizzle.

"Look!" Pat pointed. Jill saw Lucy Applebird come out the door from the rough room and down the steps, followed by a small group of elderly women. Lucy was bundled up in a shabby old coat and a small hat, but she wore a corsage on her shoulder of red, white, and blue flowers. She stood near the pole. A Boy Scout blew his trumpet, calling all to attention.

"That's Billy James," Pat said. "He's cute, isn't he."

A minister offered a prayer. One of the town's selectmen made a speech about Lucy Applebird's patriotism and how her father before her had raised the flag in the early morning and taken it down at sunset. Lucy replied in a low voice, something that Jill and Pat could not hear from their place behind the older people.

Three Boy Scouts put the new flag on ropes. They raised it while Billy James blew a salute on his trumpet. The flag fluttered in the foggy drizzle. Lucy spoke again and flash bulbs brightened the gray day. Jill shivered with emotion, it was so impressive.

Lucy began to sing "The Star-Spangled Banner," but she was too choked with happy tears to go on. A moment of embarrassed silence was broken by Jill's clear, sweet voice carrying on where Lucy left off. The little band of people and children sang with Jill right through all the rest of the stanzas.

Then a benediction was pronounced. The ceremony was over and the people hurried off in the drizzle. Many of the children ran around to the Cleaves Street store to spend their pennies.

Jill and Pat waited a few minutes. Lucy Applebird spied them beside the shed. "Jill, you were a good girl to help me out. I felt so ashamed. I was going to run off and not come back till gooseberry time. I never cry." She was angry with herself. She turned to go up the steps into the rough room, then stopped. "Jill, you have a nice voice, you ought to sing in the choir."

"Oh, no!" Jill was horrified. "I never could do that."

"Humph," snorted Lucy Applebird. "You never know till you try."

Jill and Pat parted, each to scamper home in the clinging, drizzly fog. Aunt Emma wanted to hear about the flag-raising ceremony while they ate the usual supper of baked beans.

"Your appetite is picking up." She gave Jill a second helping of beans. "Now you wash your hair after

122

the dishes are done, it's sticky with salt water and fog."

"I will," said Jill, "if you'll rub it dry." She smiled at Aunt Emma.

Aunt Emma smiled back. Jill felt warm and cosy around her heart. A smile was easy and it made her feel good, and maybe it made Aunt Emma feel good, too.

Monday, Tuesday, and Wednesday passed with no ad telling of a horse for sale. But on Thursday, when Pat delivered the paper, Jill opened it at once. She scanned the ads. There it was. She could hardly speak.

"Pat! Look!" She put her finger under an ad. Pat sat down beside her. They read it aloud together: "Friendly old pet horse. Saddle and bridle. $75. If you have a barn and a field and promise to treat her gently. Tel. Roger 8-6220."

They lifted their eyes from the ad and stared at each other. Then Pat leaped up. "WHOOPEE!" she yelled.

Aunt Emma came to the door. "What's all the racket?"

Jill showed her the ad. "Pat is going to have her horse."

Aunt Emma read the ad and was silent. Then she

123

said, "If I were you, I would phone right away before anyone else gets that horse."

Jill pushed Pat in the house and to the phone. "You must phone now and not wait till you get home after delivering the papers. It might be too late."

Pat dialed the number. A man answered. She told him she wanted to buy his horse.

He asked, "How old are you? Is your father there? I can't do business with a child."

Pat turned a troubled face to Aunt Emma. "Oh, please, tell him I have the money."

Aunt Emma made it very clear to the man that this was a responsible business deal. He agreed to bring the horse down the next day.

Pat went home in a daze after she had finished delivering papers. Her father and mother were glad to have a saddle and bridle included with the horse.

"We'll have to order some feed," her father said. "I'll show you how to care for a horse, and, remember, this is a daily duty for you. We had horses when I was a boy, and I know how much work it is."

He looked at Pat. "You'll have to learn to ride. The chap on South Street has a class. How much money will you have after paying for the horse?"

Pat was thinking. "About twenty-five dollars and, besides, I earn money every week from my paper route."

The entire family was excited at the idea of a horse coming the very next day. The stall was cleaned, and the field back of the barn was surveyed and found satisfactory. Then Joey asked, "What are you going to name your horse?"

Pat said, "I was going to name my horse Major, but this is a lady horse."

"Maybe she has a name," Elizabeth said.

"I'll wait and see," Pat said.

Jill was on hand for the arrival of the horse. She and Pat sat in front of the house impatiently waiting for the truck to appear on Summer Street. Finally it came. The driver was a pleasant man who liked the barn, liked the Wentworths, and liked Pat very much. He knew she would be kind to his horse.

He lowered the back of the truck and led out a brown horse who stepped lightly down the ramp. She clopped, with the sweetest music Pat had ever heard, into the barn. Pat's face was so bright with love and delight that it almost made Jill envy such a capacity for joy.

"Come, Beauty." The man led her into the stall.

"Beauty!" Jill cried. "That suits her, Pat."

Pat could do nothing but smile and smile. She patted Beauty's soft nose and gazed into her gentle eyes. She murmured, "Beauty . . . Beauty . . ."

The next week riding lessons were arranged and

after a few lessons the riding master was pleased with Pat's quick progress in learning to ride.

"Keep on this way and you'll enter the horse show next summer," he told her. Pat grinned down from her saddle.

The town had not heard the end of Lucy Applebird's new flag and new pole. Something had been going on secretly. She got a telegram one day, the first she had ever had. She stiffened as if to be ready for a shock. She had been told long ago that telegrams always brought bad news.

She opened it. She read it. The address and name were correct. She read on:

THROUGH CONGRESSMAN WM. H. HILL, I HAVE LEARNED OF THE TRADITIONAL FLAG-RAISING CEREMONY AT YOUR HOME IN ROCKPORT. YOUR DAILY DEMONSTRATION OF ALLEGIANCE TO THE EMBLEM OF OUR REPUBLIC IS A HEARTENING EXAMPLE TO THOSE SEEKING TO ADVANCE THE CAUSE OF LIBERTY AND JUSTICE FOR ALL.
MY BEST WISHES TO YOU AND YOUR FELLOW CITIZENS.

It was signed, and there she read the signature of the President of the United States of America.

Lucy Applebird sat in her rocking chair. She read

it again and again. She didn't know what to do, she was so shaken with the honor. She went to the window and gazed at her flag in all its beauty, rippling against the blue September sky. In no time a visitor from Town Hall, who knew all about the telegram, came to shake hands with her, and a reporter took her picture holding the telegram. Children coming to spend pennies were shown the telegram. Finally, Lucy said, "You'll wear it out, handling it."

When Jill came with Aunt Emma, who had not visited Lucy for years, Jill said, "We want you to have supper with us."

Aunt Emma was eying the shabby room. She said, "I'd be proud to have you to supper."

Lucy's eyes twinkled. She was a celebrity now, but she was not going to be stuck up about it and she said, "I'd be pleased to come." Even if Aunt Emma had always been snooty about her superior housekeeping and cooking, Lucy was fond of good food, if someone else prepared it.

September brought the opening of school. Jill was in Pat's grade. She realized that because of the fair, she knew many girls and boys, and suddenly she wasn't afraid of school. The weeks went by rapidly and fall grew into winter. Jill went to call on Lucy Applebird now and then, but school activities filled most of her spare time. She came home one day and Aunt Emma said she had some sad news for her.

"What is it? My parents?" Jill's stomach suddenly hurt, she was so frightened.

"No, Virgilia. It's poor old Lucy Applebird. She fell on her slippery steps when she was going out to raise the flag, and someone heard her cry out. The ambulance took her to the hospital."

Jill's eyes filled with tears.

"Now, Virgilia, don't cry, you can't help a bad situation with tears," Aunt Emma said.

"I want to do something for her, she was a good friend. I know, I'll raise the flag each morning and take it down at sunset," Jill announced.

"Well," Aunt Emma said, "that's not going to be easy with your schoolwork and all. But I guess the neighbors will help you out if you can't do it every day. Lucy will rest easier when she hears that her flag will be raised, I'm sure."

Sometimes when blizzards and drifted snow filled the roads, Lucy's flag was not raised, but Jill managed most days. Lucy would not come home for a long time, but she would go from the hospital to a cousin's house in Gloucester where she would be taken care of.

Jill thought it was sad to see the tiny store closed and the faded cretonne curtains pulled against the glass. The small children used to buying penny candy and the older people wanting crackers and cookies had to go down to Main Street.

Lucy Applebird was missed in the Baptist Church where she had bounced into her favorite pew ever since she was a child. And she was missed when the townspeople no longer saw her trudging through the snow to meetings, wearing her old coonskin coat that had more bare spots than fur.

Aunt Emma had given her old sleigh to Pat. And now, whenever it snowed, Beauty was hitched to it and Pat and Jill took little rides in the sleigh.

"I wish Lucy Applebird was back in her house," Jill said. "I know she would have fun riding in a sleigh."

"You are really a good friend to her. Have you been to visit her?" Pat asked.

"No," Jill admitted, "I don't seem to have time to go to Gloucester, but I want to someday. I didn't know school could be so much fun. I've never been so busy before."

Chapter Ten

Even outside school, Jill was busy. She joined a singing group that was practicing for a spring concert, and she had a solo part. Even so, she was bashful when Tommy Andrews invited her to a school dance. He joked and teased her, "Come on Jill, don't look so pained." He gave her arm a shake, "Can't you smile?" She tried a smile, and she giggled to see his grin, and she said she would go with him to the dance.

The dance was fun. She saw Pat fly by with Eric Jensen, her blond pony tail bobbing up and down. Trina was dancing with Billy James who barely came up to her shoulder. Jill loved them all. She felt a part of the school, but at recess the next day, when Pat told her that Trina had invited her to go to Boston to the theater to see the play, *Joan of Arc*, and that Trina's father would drive them there, Jill felt such a sharp pain in her heart that she gasped.

"What's the matter?" Pat asked. "You look funny."

Jill muttered, "Nothing—nothing's the matter with me." Jill couldn't stay a minute longer to hear Pat's excitement over Trina's invitation. "I've never been to Boston," she said. "I've never been in a real theater, and Trina is going to be an actress, and she is dying to see the actress who plays the part of Joan of Arc."

Jill stumbled into the schoolroom. Her stomach ached. She was so full of misery that she ran home after school without waiting for Pat. Her gloomy face brought a sharp comment from Aunt Emma. "What is the matter? You look as if you were coming down with something."

Jill didn't answer. She went up to her room. She threw her books on the bed, and herself after them. She had no clue to her misery. She pouted; she grumbled, "That silly old Trina thinks she is an actress. It isn't fair—she thinks she is beautiful because she is a blonde. It just isn't fair."

There was a knock at the door. She scowled. "Leave me alone." Her voice was a low mumble. But the door opened, and Aunt Emma came striding in. She had a thermometer in her hand.

"Here now, you roll over and let me take your temperature, Virgilia."

Jill had no choice but to open her mouth for the thermometer. Aunt Emma took her wrist to feel the pulse. Jill tried to avoid her searching eyes. Aunt Emma laid Jill's hand on the quilt and looked at the thermometer. "Your temperature is normal and so is your pulse. There is so much flu going around I was worried."

Jill pouted and twitched away from Aunt Emma's hands.

"Look here, young lady." Aunt Emma was stern. "You tell me what's on your mind. Something is bothering you. What is it?"

Jill shrugged her shoulders and started to roll out the far side of the wide bed, but Aunt Emma held her back. "Tell me, Virgilia."

Jill's lips trembled. Her throat ached, and then tears came to her eyes while Aunt Emma smoothed back her tumbled hair. Jill wept noisily.

"Now, now," Aunt Emma's salty voice crooned. "Now, now, it can't be so awful. What is troubling you?"

Jill choked out the words, "Pat is going to Boston."

"Well, what of it?" Aunt Emma said.

"She is going with that Trina Jensen who thinks she is going to be a famous actress," Jill blubbered.

Aunt Emma's voice was relieved. "Virgilia, you have a plain case of jealousy. I bet your eyes have turned green with jealousy."

Jill sobbed, "It hurts."

133

"Of course," Aunt Emma agreed. "I suppose at home you just stayed in your room and sulked. Your parents let you indulge yourself in self-pity. They didn't help you to overcome your jealousy. It can get to be a bad habit if you don't watch out."

"I didn't know I was jealous," Jill wept. "But Pat is my best friend and I never had a best friend before."

Aunt Emma was brisk. "Sit up, Virgilia. Let me tell you something about jealousy that I learned long ago. First, tell me, you love Pat, don't you?"

Jill nodded, "Yes."

"Do you like to see her happy?" Aunt Emma asked.

"Yes," Jill faltered.

Aunt Emma nodded with energy. "And you wouldn't want to take away something that made her happy, would you?"

"No," Jill slowly admitted.

"Well then, what is troubling you?" Aunt Emma's voice probed into Jill's mind, and made her think. She thought seriously about it, and finally she said, "I guess I don't want Pat to be happy with Trina."

Aunt Emma was silent. Jill went on digging into her feelings. "I guess . . . I guess that it is being selfish when you want to keep somebody you love from having something nice happen to them."

Jill's eyes began to brighten, and she looked at

Aunt Emma with a sense of discovery. It was hard to express what was in her mind. She made an effort. "I tried to own Pat. You can't own people, can you, Aunt Emma?"

"My lands, no," Aunt Emma chuckled. She leaned over to pick up Jill's schoolbooks. "What is this book about, *The Egg Tree?*"

Jill said, "It is a library book I have to read, and write a review about it for next week. I have lots of homework."

Aunt Emma stood up and went to the door. She turned to give Jill a last word. "Keep busy, that's my prescription."

Jill tackled her homework. She read *The Egg Tree*, and she learned how children in Europe had made egg trees at Easter. It was a fascinating book. When Aunt Emma called her to supper, she put it down reluctantly.

The next day was Saturday, and Aunt Emma said that she had work for Jill. "You can rake up the old leaves under the bushes. The yard must be neat for Easter. Pile them in those bushel baskets back of the woodshed where the rubbish collector can find them."

Jill raked the soggy old leaves into piles and filled the baskets. There were old rotten apples under the trees, and she filled a basket with them. She picked

135

up a branch that had broken off during a storm and held it up. It was shaped like a perfect small tree. She couldn't bear to break it up, and she stuck it into some soft earth back of the shed. "I wish you could grow and be a young apple tree," she said to the branch.

Aunt Emma called from the kitchen door, "Dinner is almost ready. You've done a fine job, Virgilia. Come in and get washed up."

Jill's appetite was good. The fresh air and hard work had made her eyes sparkle, and there was a rosy tinge on her cheeks.

"This afternoon we are going to Gloucester to shop," Aunt Emma announced. "Your mother sent the money for a new hat and new shoes for you, and I need some things, too. Let's hurry with the dishes so we can catch the one-thirty bus."

Jill and Aunt Emma jogged along in the bus past Five Corners up Great Hill. The woods on one side and the pastures on the other side showed signs of spring leaves. The bare trees in the distance were no longer gray, but a warm, pinkish color, and the sky was all blue without a cloud in sight. The pastures were still shaggy and rumpled with the old, long tawny grass; green was slower to appear on the ground.

Aunt Emma said, "I heard the peepers last night, did you?"

"No," Jill turned from the window. "I have never heard peepers. What does it sound like?"

Aunt Emma hesitated, "Well, come to think of it, they sound like little jingling bells coming from a distance. We'll listen for them; there is no sound that makes you think spring is coming like those little fellows peeping in the swampy places."

The bus turned into Main Street where they met with huge refrigerator trucks maneuvering with traffic on their way to the fish-freezing plants on the waterfront. They got off near a big department store, and Jill soon found herself trying on straw hats. She liked a white sailor with a turned-up brim and red streamers best of all. Aunt Emma said, "My, it's kind of plain. . . ."

The salesgirl piped up, "But it is smart." She caught Jill's eyes in the mirror, and they exchanged an understanding grin.

The hat was put into a box, and they proceeded to the shoe department. Jill was fitted with shiny black flats, and Aunt Emma selected stout black Oxfords with sensible heels. She bought three yards of blue-checked gingham for a new apron, and then declared herself in need of a cup of coffee. She guided Jill to

137

the basement floor and the lunch counter. "What would you like—a cup of cocoa?"

"No, thank you," Jill said. "I'll browse in the book department while you have your coffee."

Jill read the titles of books for young readers; some sounded interesting, especially *The Smugglers of Sandy Bay*. She was surprised when a girl's voice cried out, "Jill, Jill!"

She turned and saw a girl from her class. "Hi!" she said. It was Debbie Norton who had been in the play *Little Women* that the Girl Scouts had put on.

Debbie chattered, "Wasn't Pat lucky to go to Boston to see a real play in a real theater with Trina? She is going to be an actress, Trina is."

Jill felt a stab somewhere near her heart. For a moment she was silent. Then she drew a deep breath and said steadily, "It's wonderful that Pat had the chance to go to a real play with Trina. I'm sure she had a fine time."

The words came out of her mouth, and the sound of them strengthened her. She could just picture Pat's happy, radiant face. Pat had a way of enjoying things deeply and thoroughly.

"Be seeing you," Debbie cried, and ran to catch up with her mother.

Aunt Emma found Jill smiling and talking to the clerk about books. They had to hurry out to catch the bus for home. Jill was eager to hear from Pat all about her visit to Boston. But when she phoned, Mrs. Wentworth said Pat was in bed with a heavy cold and such a sore throat that she couldn't speak. "I'll have to keep her in bed a week, the doctor says. Easter is next Sunday, and with school vacation coming she will have to get someone to take her paper route." She hesitated, "Jill, do you think you could take her paper route? I'll go around with you the first day to help you find her customers."

Jill hastened to say, "Oh, no, I could never do that. Good-by."

Jill hung up in a panic. The idea of delivering papers and collecting the money at the end of the week was too much to even think about. How could she ever join the noisy boys at the waiting station where each boy picked up his pack of Gloucester *Daily Times*. She knew they poked fun at Pat's doll buggy. They drank Cokes. They munched potato chips and crunched ice-cream cones down to the last crumb. They were always hungry, always rough, and always teasing and punching each other. Pat did not mind it. Sometimes Jill thought she liked it. She laughed and went about her business with a broad grin. Jill was pensive. "I suppose Pat would call me a baby and a scaredy cat. She will be disappointed and probably worry because no one would help her out . . . she needs help . . . now."

Jill made herself go to the phone. She spoke to Mrs. Wentworth. "Tell Pat that I will take her route," she mumbled.

"What's that?" Mrs. Wentworth asked anxiously.

Jill breathed deeply. "Tell Pat that I will take her paper route."

Mrs. Wentworth cried, "Oh, thank you, Jill. Shall I send the doll buggy down to you by a neighbor?"

Jill did not like to think of herself pushing that rickety old doll buggy up and down the streets but she realized it would be a great help on hilly streets. She said, "Yes, please."

Mrs. Wentworth was relieved. "Just wait till I tell Pat; she is so worried and so sick and can't say a word. . . . Good-by, and thank you, Jill."

Jill sat down to stare out the window. She didn't feel very good. She was worried.

Chapter Eleven

Jill did not look forward to Monday, and she kept wishing it would never come. But it did come and she did go to the waiting station with the doll buggy. There was the usual crowd of boys, and they stopped eating potato chips and ice-cream cones, and they stopped drinking Cokes. "For Pete's sake, look who's here with the doll buggy!" one boy shouted.

"Hey," another boy jeered, "here's Pat's pony express!"

Jill went to the pile of papers. "Which one is Pat's?" she asked a boy she had seen in school. He pointed it out.

"Where is Pat?" he asked.

Jill said, "She is too sick to take her papers, and I'm doing it for her."

"Golly," another boy said to her. "You're a good

kid. Here, I'll put the papers in the buggy. If you need any help, ask me or any of the gang."

"Sure," they all chimed in.

Jill thanked them and pushed the buggy out with its load of papers. She looked at the list of houses Mrs. Wentworth had given her, and she started on her way. Pat's mother met her at the library and went the rest of the route with her until Jill was sure of her locations, and then she left Jill and went home to tend to her family.

The early spring afternoon grew cold and a raw wind sprang up. Jill got tired before all the papers were delivered, and she wondered why Pat had never complained about the work being tiresome. Jill thought how Pat went through all kinds of weather to see that her customers got their Gloucester *Daily Times*. When she finally came home with the doll buggy and the paper for Aunt Emma, she plopped into the kitchen rocker with a groan. "Golly," she moaned. No wonder the paper boys stoked up on chips and ice cream before they carried their papers around the town. She wondered if she had enough strength to get a cooky from the pantry. She got up slowly and found there was a batch of fresh sugar cookies in the stone crock. She took one, and then she took another.

Rocking and munching and relaxing she shut her

eyes and not until she heard Aunt Emma come in the front door and into the kitchen did she open them. Aunt Emma was full of news gathered at the meeting of the Ladies' Friendship Society.

"They say the town has got to build a new school because the population is exploding," she said. "Think what that will do to raise our taxes! Some of the women with large families are all in favor of it, and because they live in rented houses, they don't pay taxes. I don't see why I should have to pay more taxes because I own my home and I don't have children in school. It's all I can do now to keep up my property. . . ." Aunt Emma sputtered as she banged a frying pan on the stove. She scrubbed carrots and potatoes until their skins came off, she was in such a frenzy of injustice.

Jill watched her in astonishment. She had never seen Aunt Emma mad as a wet hen. Jill wondered what she could say to calm her.

"These are very good cookies," she ventured. "Extra good . . . I think . . . the best I ever ate . . ." Her voice faltered.

Aunt Emma switched around from the sink, and her tall, angular figure began to relax. "That is a new recipe with a bit of mace and grated lemon rind in the dough. It took a prize in that big baking contest in California. The woman won a complete electric

145

kitchen and a trip to California with all expenses paid."

"Golly," Jill exclaimed with relief to see Aunt Emma acting like herself again.

Aunt Emma looked surprised. "You got your papers at the waiting station, and you picked up that vulgar word from those rude boys who talk that way. I don't know what your parents will think."

Jill protested, "They were so nice to me and helped me, and even if they do say, 'golly,' I like to say it, too."

"Well—well," Aunt Emma's voice petered out. "There are worse words to say, I guess."

After supper Jill did her homework. But she was so tired she found it hard to keep her eyes open. At last she closed the books and the notebooks, and slid into bed. Her sleep was deep and dreamless.

At breakfast Aunt Emma confessed that she had been unreasonable about the town's need for a new school. "Times have changed. I don't want to be a stick-in-the-mud. People have to change along with the times."

Jill nodded absent-mindedly. Aunt Emma's words didn't penetrate her mind because it was buzzing with an idea. She was thinking about Pat's being sick in bed unable to talk or to go out, and outdoors, spring was growing lovelier by the hour. The tiny

146

leaves burst out on the bare bushes and the grass was pale, young, and green. There was a good smell of grass and of softening earth in the gardens. She was silent so long that Aunt Emma spoke up, "Aren't you hungry? You'd better finish your breakfast. Look at the clock. You'll be late for school."

Jill grinned at her. "I'll finish in a jiffy. When I come home from school, I have a plan to talk over with you." Then she remembered the paper route. "After supper I'll ask your advice."

The paper route was a little easier because she knew each house now without looking for the numbers. The boys were helpful and jolly, and she didn't mind their teasing. After supper Jill asked Aunt Emma, "How much are eggs a dozen?"

Aunt Emma was on her way to the TV set, and she turned back in amazement.

"Eggs? Why do you want to know?" she asked.

Jill explained, "I'm going to buy two dozen eggs with my allowance." And then she giggled to see Aunt Emma's bewildered expression.

"I'm going to make an egg tree," Jill went on to explain.

"Egg tree? For pity's sake, what is that?" Aunt Emma gave all her attention to Jill.

"You see, in Germany long ago, the people made

egg trees, and when those people came to America, they kept on making egg trees."

Aunt Emma nodded, "Sounds reasonable enough. Where did the Germans settle?"

Jill said, "The book says in the Pennsylvania-Dutch country."

Aunt Emma was enjoying herself, and she questioned Jill as if she were a schoolteacher. "And why do the people make egg trees at Easter?"

Jill had to giggle. "The colors symbolize the return of color after the long, drab winter, and the egg symbolizes new life and resurrection."

Aunt Emma added, "And it is a symbol of spring! Now, tell me how you go about this business."

"You pierce the egg at each end with a darning needle, and one end is a bit larger than the other. You blow in the small end and the insides come out leaving an empty shell."

Aunt Emma spoke up, "You don't let the insides go to waste, I hope. It seems to me we'll have scrambled eggs and custards and eggnogs for days."

Jill thought of all the egg dishes she would have to eat. It did not seem very appetizing, but then she was doing this for Pat. It was to be a surprise on Easter morning.

Aunt Emma said, "Eggs are seventy-two cents a dozen. Have you enough money?"

Jill ran up to her room to look in her purse. She had $1.25. She came down and said shyly, "Would you lend me nineteen cents until I get my next allowance?"

Aunt Emma said she would. "But aren't you going to color the eggs? You'll need money to buy a package of Easter-egg dyes. I'll lend you enough for that, and I'll get the eggs when I go shopping in the morning and the dyes, too."

The next evening Jill started to blow out the eggs. It wasn't as easy as it said in the book, and two eggs broke into smithereens.

Aunt Emma told her to put the bowls of egg yolks and whites in the refrigerator. "What are you going to use for the tree?" she asked Jill.

"I found a broken branch from the apple tree, and I put it in back of the shed. If you have a large flowerpot I can use, it will stand up like a real tree." Jill looked at her sticky fingers. The egg shells were sticky, too, and she filled a basin with warm water and gently washed and dried the shells.

Aunt Emma had gone down cellar, and she came up holding a fancy jardiniere. "I used to have an umbrella plant in this jardiniere. They seem to have gone out of style. Would you like to use it for the egg tree?"

"Oh, yes," Jill cried. "It's perfect. I'm sure my

branch will fit it. Now I have homework to do before I go to bed." She placed the egg shells in the egg boxes and put them in the pantry. She was delighted with the way her egg tree was working out.

The next morning Jill got up early and began dyeing the egg shells. It was a drippy, messy job, but by Friday she had deep-purple eggs, red eggs, blue eggs, yellow and orange eggs, and some were as green as shamrocks. Aunt Emma admired them. "When I was little, we used scraps of calico tied around the eggs and then we boiled them, and the color came off on the eggs. Sometimes the tiny designs on the calico were printed on the eggs. We had some Greek neighbors, and the children had only red-colored eggs, and they cracked them against each other's eggs and one said, 'Christ is risen!' and the other replied, 'He is risen indeed.' They said it in Greek, but they told us the meaning." Aunt Emma went on, "They belonged to the family that has the handsome grocery store down on Broadway."

Jill was interested. "I wonder if Father and Mother will be in Greece for Easter. I read that their Easter isn't at the same time as ours. It's a bit later."

Aunt Emma spoke up, "You haven't had a letter for quite a while, seems to me. They must be traveling most of the time and learning a lot, too." Aunt Emma nodded her head vigorously. "You are learning a lot, too, just living in this town. We have a good library and good schoolteachers. I didn't realize that until you came to live with me." She chuckled, "Live and learn. I guess that is true for me. I'm in favor of a new school, now that I've given it some thought."

All week while she dyed eggs, Jill planned how to surprise Pat.

"I'll take it to her house on Saturday after dark and put it outside her window so she can see it first thing Easter morning," she said to herself.

Friday, Jill collected the money for the Gloucester *Daily Times*. On Saturday morning she delivered the early morning edition. Then she put the little tree in the jardiniere and packed earth around it firmly so it stood up securely. She smiled to herself remembering how she had wished it would grow into a real tree the day she was cleaning and raking the yard. "My wish came true in a very surprising way, I never dreamed it would have colored eggs on it instead of apples!"

She brought it in and placed it on the kitchen table. She threaded strong linen thread through the eggs and tied them on the branches. She hummed contentedly, and said to herself, "I love apple blossoms best of all flowers." She peered out the window at the apple tree with its budding green leaves. "I

hope Pat will be well for Easter vacation so she can ride Beauty." On and on, Jill dreamed and planned what good times she would have with Pat. Aunt Emma had said that she could invite Pat for supper some evening. "I'll invite Trina, too," Jill decided. "I can't keep Pat all for myself, and she likes Trina . . . and I like Trina, too. . . ." She was firm with herself.

The daylight faded away in a lemon-yellow sky with touches of gold around the low sunset clouds. It was going to be a lovely, clear Easter Day. As soon as it was dark, Jill put the egg tree in the doll buggy and put tissue paper over it so that no one could see what she was trundling through the streets. There was hardly a soul to be seen. She came to the Wentworth house and pushed the buggy to the side of the house. The little tree was placed under Pat's window. To Jill's dismay she found it was too close to the ground and that Pat would not be able to see it from the window when she woke and looked out to see what the day was going to be.

Jill was thoughtful. "I'll have to put it on a box; but where will I get a box?"

She glanced around nervously. "Maybe I can find one in the barn." She tiptoed to the back of the house and across the yard, opened a small side door, and looked in. It was quite dark, with only a little light

153

from two cobwebby windows. She heard Beauty stamp her feet and make little nickering noises.

Jill was afraid to get near Beauty. She tiptoed fearfully toward a pile of boxes and old lumber. She felt around in the dim light, and just as she was pulling a box from the heap, she heard the side door opening. Panic shook her and she slipped into the stall next to Beauty's stall. She pulled herself up and then crouched down in the manger. Jill's heart was beating so fast she thought she would die. She heard someone walk into the barn. She was sure it was a burglar planning to steal Beauty. She had her face pressed down in the dusty manger. Her nose tickled, and she started to sneeze, but before it came out full and hearty she choked it back.

"Who's there?" a voice asked.

She was too frightened to even squeak. The sound of a person walking on the rough floor came closer. Jill squeezed herself into a tiny ball, frozen with fear.

"Move over, Beauty, old girl," the voice said. "I'm going to take some of your hay to fill the children's Easter baskets."

Jill heard a hearty slap on Beauty's back and a rumbling of hoofs and a soft nickering from the horse. It was Pat's father talking to the horse. But before Jill could get her voice working again and before she could stop trembling, the barn door closed.

Jill clutched the rough boards and scrambled out. Her hand hurt, but she didn't stop to look at it. She picked up the box and crept around the house. She placed the egg tree on the box. It glimmered faintly in the soft spring starlight. It was right where Pat would see it first thing on Easter morning. She pushed the doll buggy home. Her hand really hurt, and it was bleeding a little.

When Aunt Emma asked Jill what had happened, Jill held up her hand. There was a jagged sliver in the palm. Aunt Emma tried to pull it out, but some bits were too deeply imbedded for her probing needle to reach. Jill wriggled away from her with squeals of "Ouch, ouch!"

"I'll make a warm bread-and-milk poultice for it, and tie it on after you have had your bath. Then I'll wash your hair so you'll be all fresh and clean for Easter." Aunt Emma took out two slices of bread and laid them on the table, ready to crumble into enough hot milk to make a paste.

Jill went to bed sweet and clean with her hand done up in a bulky bandage around the poultice. She slept well and woke on Easter morning remembering what Pat would be looking at and how she would cry out with surprise.

After breakfast the phone rang, and Mrs. Wentworth told Jill that Pat was wrapped up in a blanket and waiting to talk to her. "Don't talk long, Jill. Her voice is still quite hoarse," she warned.

"Oh, Jill!" Pat croaked. "I never saw anything so beautiful in all my life! How did you ever think of making such . . . such . . ."

Jill broke in, "Egg tree, Pat. I read about it in a book, but golly, if you knew how many eggs I have eaten, you'd expect me to grow feathers!"

Pat's laughter was a series of croaks and moans; she finally said, "You'll grow wings because you are an angel, Jill. But don't fly away!"

Jill giggled. They could say no more because Mrs. Wentworth broke in. "That's all for today, girls. But wait, Jill, someone else wants to talk to you." Jill waited.

"Hi, Jill, you had me scared last night when I came into the barn and heard a noise. Why didn't you speak up?" It was Mr. Wentworth.

Jill mumbled, "I was too scared. I didn't know it was you until you told Beauty you wanted some hay. I was embarrassed to be hiding in the manger. I thought you were a burglar trying to steal Beauty. I was a coward not to try to save her."

"Come, come, Jill. I don't think you were a coward to go in that dark barn alone, and I'm sure you would have tackled a burglar with those mighty muscles of yours."

That statement made Jill choke with giggles. Her skinny arms were not muscular. They ended the chat, and Jill turned to see Aunt Emma eying the clock. She said they must get dressed for church and be there early because many people, who did not go to church except on Christmas and Easter, would fill the pews.

Jill walked sedately with Aunt Emma down the village street, her white sailor hat with its red ribbons perched becomingly on her shining, long brown hair. Jill thought that the church bells chimed with more than their usual joy, and the faces of the churchgoers seemed to have a special glow. The Easter story was an old one, but it was always new and wonderful each year.

Easter vacation was busy. Jill kept on with Pat's paper route and she was delighted to hand over the collection to her. As soon as Pat could come outdoors, Aunt Emma prepared a supper for the girls. Jill had asked for chicken salad with Parker House rolls and potato chips and olives. There was an Easter-special ice cream sold at the waiting station, and they had that for dessert. Trina was there, and she entertained them all by acting out the part of Joan of Arc being burned at the stake. She was so dramatic that it made Jill shiver.

Jill's hand was sore. The poultice hadn't pulled all

the slivers out, and Aunt Emma took Jill to see Dr. Greene. He said bread-and-milk poultices did not help much, but they did no harm. He looked at Jill's hand through powerful glasses, and in a jiffy he had the slivers out. He painted the spot with some red medicine that had a sting to it, and gave her some to take home. "Keep your hand clean and put this disinfectant on it a couple of times and it will be healed."

Jill watched him open a drawer and take out a lollipop. "I guess you aren't too old for a lollipop. I give them to all my young patients."

Aunt Emma paid his bill, and they went out and down the steps onto Broadway. She said, "Some of the younger doctors don't want to make calls at night, but that good man is never too tired or too modern to help out folks any time of the day or night."

"He is nice, and he didn't hurt—well, not much," Jill said.

Aunt Emma had some letters to mail at the post office a few doors away. "I wonder why we don't hear from your parents," she said. Jill hardly heard her. Vacation was over, and she was thinking about school again. She felt so much a part of the school that later that week, when Aunt Emma had a letter from Jill's father telling the date of his return, Jill felt a real pang somewhere near her heart. She realized that she didn't want to leave Rockport.

Chapter Twelve

The time had come for her parents to return from Europe. Aunt Emma teased, "What a long face, Virgilia. Listen to what I am going to tell you."

Jill eyed Aunt Emma anxiously.

"The long and short of it is, your father is buying the Applebird house." She watched to see what effect that news would have. Jill's mouth dropped open. She could not even squeak, she was so surprised. Aunt Emma went on, "Lucy Applebird decided to sell her house, but not to anyone she did not approve of. She cannot live alone, so she will stay in Gloucester. Of course your father hasn't much money to spend for a house, but I went to the bank to see about a mortgage and other details. The banker knew your father when they were boys, and the Stewarts are good, honest folks. So it was arranged.

Your father has made a down payment. The house is large, and an apartment will be made on the lower floor facing Jewett Street to rent the year around. That takes care of the mortgage and taxes that have to be paid."

She looked at Jill. "Well, Virgilia, can't you say something?"

Jill found her voice. "What about the store? Will we keep a store?"

Aunt Emma said, "I knew you'd ask that. But the rooms on the Cleaves Street side are to be used summers only by you and your parents. They have to go back to teaching, you know. About the store, your mother will have that for an art gallery. It is real handy for folks to drop by and look at her exhibition and perhaps buy her paintings. The rough room will be made into a modern kitchen and lots of painting and papering will be done in all the rooms. The place has been neglected many years. Lucky thing the roof is new since the hurricane."

Jill thought of Lucy's tower room and its secret. She realized that she had not thought much about Lucy lately. She recalled how Lucy had laughed at her timidity. "She understands me," Jill mused. "She helped me to learn how to be friendly and to smile a lot. I'm not lonely any more."

Aunt Emma waited for Jill to get over the big sur-

prise before telling her that she was going to take her to Gloucester in a few days to visit Lucy. "It will be her birthday," she said.

"I want to give her a present," Jill said. "What would be nice? What would she like, Aunt Emma?"

"You give that some thought, Virgilia. Give her something straight from your heart." Aunt Emma left the room to begin supper.

Jill thought and thought about the present. At last she knew what she could give Lucy Applebird, straight from her heart.

The Gloucester bus took them to Middle Street where they got off and walked to a large old-fashioned home. They were greeted by a pleasant white-haired lady who cried out, "Emma Harris, I declare. And isn't this Virgilia Stewart?"

She held out her hand to shake each of theirs and drew them into the front parlor. There was Lucy Applebird in a wheel chair receiving her birthday visitors. Jill was sorry to see her looking thin and worn and pale, but her eyes were bright and her hello was the same as ever. "Well, Jill, let's have a visit." She motioned to Jill to sit beside her. Jill answered all her questions about school and the fun she was having.

"Putting on some flesh, I see." Lucy leaned over and pinched Jill's rosy cheek. "You're growing into a pretty girl. You don't have that lost and forlorn orphan look any more."

Jill smiled. "Thank you for being such a good friend to me when I first came to Rockport. You were my first friend!"

Lucy whispered, "I'm going to give you my telegram from our President one of these days. You have it framed and hang it in your bedroom. I hope you take the room I had as a girl. It looked across Jewett Street to Town Hall."

Jill nodded. "I will, and I'll always think of you and the flag and . . ."

"Hush," Lucy whispered. "You just forget our secret. It is forgotten by me."

Before the conversation grew sad, there was a birthday cake covered with so many glittering candles that no one wanted to count them. After the ice cream was passed, Lucy Applebird opened her gifts. She got a parakeet to teach, and many plants and flowers. Aunt Emma gave her a box of fudge and she wondered what Virgilia was giving, until Jill stood up during a pause and spoke out. Her voice was low and trembly, but it gained steadiness and confidence. She said, "I am going to sing a song for your birthday present."

Jill began: "By yon bonnie banks,/And by yon bonnie braes,/Where the sun shines bright on Loch

164

Lomond,/Where me and my true love/Were ever wont to gae,/On the bonnie, bonnie banks of Loch Lomond./Oh! ye'll take the high road and I'll take the low road,/And I'll be in Scotland afore ye;/But me and my true love will never meet again/On the bonnie, bonnie banks of Loch Lomond."

Lucy Applebird fumbled for her handkerchief. Only she and Jill knew the sorrow of that old Scottish song and its meaning for a long-ago romance.

The party broke up. On the bus going home, Aunt Emma remarked, "Why did you choose that song, Virgilia?" Her eyes were sharp and probing.

Jill said, "Oh—because . . ." she faltered, "because . . ."

"Never mind, Virgilia." Aunt Emma's voice was very kind and soft. "Never mind, my girl. You sang very well."

Jill smiled. "Thank you Aunt Emma. I'd like to join the choir in your church." She saw Aunt Emma's face turn pink with pleasure.

The day came when school was over and vacation began, and Jill saw from the calendar that she had been in Rockport a year. Soon, her parents would come to spend the summer fixing up the Applebird house. Pat and Jill planned picnics and swimming parties. Pat was ready for the horse show. "I wish you liked horses," she told Jill.

"I'll be there to see you win honors," Jill promised. "Maybe my mother and father will come, too."

Pat said, "I can't get used to your having a mother and father here. I thought maybe they didn't love you."

"Oh, they do love me, but I used to feel unwanted." Jill was serious. "I'm going to have fun with them. I'm going to love them more and be part of a family, like your family, Pat. I'm going to be so proud to show them that I have a best friend."

Pat laughed. "Wait till they see how you have changed, you were so scared of me."

Jill giggled. "It doesn't seem possible, but I was."

The meeting with her mother and father was very happy. Jill looked at her tall, slender father with his unruly mop of dark hair and his studious absent-minded eyes. Usually he had a faraway look, but today his eyes were sparkling and fascinated with what he saw when he stared at Jill.

Her mother was still the small, gentle woman who was always losing her scarves or her gloves or umbrellas—but who never mislaid her painting equipment.

They hugged and kissed her and said how much they had missed her and that they would never leave her again for such a long time.

166

"I think we have been so wrapped up in our work that we neglected you and left you out." Jill's mother patted her hair.

"How thick and shiny your hair has become, and you have grown at least an inch or more."

Jill told her how Aunt Emma rubbed it dry after a shampoo and brushed it. She told how Aunt Emma made her cat. "I like chowder too, and I go out to get the haddock from Charlie Nelson's truck, and a white dog, named Babo, sits on the seat. The cats come running for fish scraps when they see the truck."

Her parents smiled and smiled to hear her happy chatter.

"Mother, do you know the Gloucester *Daily Times* has ads for kittens to be adopted? Some have double paws, too."

"Virgilia, are you hinting?" Her mother laughed.

"Mother, can't you call me Jill? Everybody except Aunt Emma calls me Jill," she begged.

Her father laughed. "Of course we can. I wonder now what the boys called that old Italian for short. You were named for Publius Vergilius Maro. Would they call him Pub or Verg? A poor joke, forget it."

Jill glanced from her father to her mother. They were all laughing and having fun together. She asked if they had the key to the Applebird house and if they would let her show it to them.

"We have the key," her father said. "You take us on a guided tour, the way they show houses in Europe."

Jill walked between them down Cleaves Street. She wore a happy expression. She was part of a family, and she was part of Rockport, at least every summer. She would have her best friend, Pat, waiting for the winter to pass so they could have vacation together. She would raise the flag for Lucy Applebird every day, and she would make new friends at home, for now she knew that if she wanted friends she would have to do her part and be a friend.

E49